Adult Teeth

Adult Teeth

Short Stories

Jeremy T. Wilson

Tortoise Books
Chicago, IL

FIRST EDITION, OCTOBER 2018

©2018 Jeremy T. Wilson

Published in the United States by Tortoise Books.
www.tortoisebooks.com

ISBN-10: 1-948954-01-X
ISBN-13: 978-1-948954-01-3

Cover design by Bryan Perry.
Tortoise Books Logo Copyright ©2018 by Tortoise Books. Original artwork by Rachele O'Hare.

Table of Contents

Welcome to Gorilla City

Somebody had been putting animals on the water towers. A giraffe at Simmons Park. A hippo out on the highway. A silverback gorilla on the biggest and most visible tower, the one painted with the town's greeting in bold green letters: "WELCOME TO CHARITY." The gorilla was hunched over, knuckles dragging, its enormous black body hiding the letters *h*, *a*, and *r*.

"Welcome to Gorilla City," she said. "Get it?"

He didn't laugh.

They were driving to his mom's to pick up the girls. The girls loved the animals like she did. They tried to guess what would be next. Bea wanted a black stallion. Lizzy wanted a bunny, a big white bunny with candy eggs, and inside those eggs more candy eggs, and inside those candy eggs more candy eggs. Sara chose not to tell them that the town had run out of water towers or that the animals were jungle-themed and not farm-themed. Best to let their imaginations run wild. If there had been another blank water tower, Sara would've wanted to see an elephant.

At dinner Jake had told her to prepare for the worst. She had told him that the worst wasn't coming. He'd said it was. She'd said it wasn't, and it wasn't because reality can and will make things worse than we can imagine. "So how can we prepare for the worst when the worst is always waiting?"

"What's worse than prison?" he'd asked.

"They'll probably let you play golf there, like one of those Martha Stewart prisons. Maybe you'll meet Martha Stewart."

"Martha Stewart is free."

"Good. I love Martha Stewart."

The girls were curled up on the couch with their MeMu, the three of them watching a movie in the dark. Sara couldn't tell what the movie was, some cartoon, so it was probably okay. Sometimes Jake's mom let them watch age-inappropriate movies, movies she wanted to watch, but she always took the girls with less than a moment's notice, so how could Sara complain? The girls begged to stay until the movie was over. Jake hopped on the couch and burrowed in with all of them. There was no more room, so Sara went into the kitchen and uncorked her mother-in-law's half-drunk bottle of chardonnay and poured it in a juice glass. She stared at two bowls of barely eaten shrimp salad dotted with coarse grounds of pepper. The girls would be hungry on the way home.

"The capital of Alabama is Montgomery," Bea said. "The capital of Alaska is Juneau. The capital of Arkansas is Little Rock."

"You skipped Arizona," Sara said.

"Crap. Phoenix."

"Where are we going?" Lizzy asked.

Sara had taken a wrong turn on the way to school. She wanted to get a closer look at the gorilla. She didn't know how much longer he would be there, and she wanted them all to appreciate him before he was gone.

"A surprise," she said.

"I have a quiz," Bea said.

"You won't miss it."

Sara drove as close to the water tower as she could get, the parking lot of a nearby storage garage, and the three of them got out and walked. It was a good morning for looking up, the sky a dull and solid slate gray. The gorilla was huge. He wasn't the King Kong type, not baring his sharp white gorilla teeth and clutching a blond beauty, but an accurate naturalistic depiction of a gorilla.

"How'd he get up there?" Lizzy asked.

"He climbed, I guess."

"He's not real," Bea said.

Sara wondered who could've done it. What kind of person had thought that sticking jungle animals to the sides of water towers was something to do? Did he—or she—have any deeper meaning behind it or was it just a joke, as Jake had said? He hardly gave the gorilla any thought, which bothered Sara. Someone had brought into existence something that yesterday wasn't there and tomorrow would probably be gone. There was something beautiful about that.

Bea pointed up to the tower and smiled. "Welcome to Gorilla City," she said.

Lizzy laughed and lifted her arms to the sky. "I get it!"

Jake's dad owned a trucking and construction empire and had done very, very well for himself. He'd been a major fundraising force for the former governor of Georgia, a childhood friend, who was now serving six and a half years for using state funds for personal travel with expensive escorts. The governor had also converted a secluded barrier island into a publicly funded yet entirely private hunter's paradise filled with wild game. Jake's dad had shot a gnu there. When the investigation started, Jake's dad turned whistle-blower. He claimed he had no choice. He said he couldn't afford to have the government poking its nose into his family business. Shortly after, his dad died of a massive heart attack at the age of sixty-one. The guilt of betraying his long-time friend had killed him. The guilt and the weight. Jake wasn't fat like his dad, thank God. "Don't take this the wrong way," Sara said the first time she met Jake's dad, "but he reminds me of Boss Hogg."

Jake smiled. "He is both those things."

Jake became the honest and youthful face of the company, and this had turned out well for the whole family until a recent spate of bad luck. The company had once built a mid-rise retirement development on the coast in Brunswick, and that structure was now slowly sinking into the salt marsh. A local TV hack charged with investigating the frequent and more prevalent cracks in the building's walls had suggested that Jake's dad, who was still alive at the time of design and construction, had known all along about this potential risk. Jake didn't really think this was all that big of a deal. They could shore it up. But part two of the investigation, which aired one night later, also discovered that the ground water was contaminated, and someone else's MeMu and PePu had been soaking their gardens and taking their meds with water toxic enough to catch fire. The visuals for the news were stunning. A woman in a floral housecoat stood next to her roses and let the news hack flick a lighter below the shower from her watering can. Fireworks. Jake thought the company could weather this storm too, but he was worried about what they'd find next, what other dirt a deeper investigation might turn up, a real investigation, not one taken on by a crusading local TV journalist with big TV dreams. That's when he confessed to Sara about the trucks and what they'd been carrying back from Florida for years.

"Don't they get hot in there?" she asked. They were in bed. The lights were out, the TV off, the girls asleep, the house quiet.

"These people don't know hot."

"Everybody knows hot."

"They're used to it."

"What's wrong with the people already here?"

"Are you going to pick peaches?"

"I probably could if I had to."

"You might have to."

"I could."

"I know. As an enlightened dude I see that you work very hard every day at keeping the house together, raising our daughters, et cetera, et cetera, but that's not the same thing as picking peaches."

"At least I'd get paid."

"A mother's reward is the future."

"I'd rather have a pocketbook."

They were both silent for a while. She thought he'd fallen asleep. He grabbed her hand under the covers, slid his fingers inside her fingers. "You won't have to pick peaches," he said. "We'll move. We'll take Mom with us. The cost of living in Costa Rica is, like, nothing."

"I don't want the girls to grow up in Costa Rica," she said.

"They like the beach. You like the beach."

"You're not serious."

"How about Nebraska?" he asked, and kissed her bare shoulder.

The capital of Nebraska is Lincoln, she thought.

He was just some high school kid messing around, but his messing around had gotten him on the news. They didn't want to release his name or give him too much individual attention for fear of copycats and undeserved fame. So the news touted him as "The Water Tower Zoologist" and blurred over his school picture so all you could see was an open shirt collar and a gold rope chain around a white neck. Sara didn't think this was quite the right name for him. He wasn't really a zoologist, but the news could never be counted on to get anything right.

At first Sara was embarrassed to find out the person responsible for the animals was just a kid, that a kid in a gold rope chain had moved her, that a teenage boy's idea of a joke had made such an impact on her, but she got over it when she found out there was more to what he'd been doing. According to the internet, the technique was called wheatpasting, and it was a popular form of graffiti in bigger cities like Chicago and New York. The kids who did this were legitimate and well-respected artists. They had websites and Twitter accounts telling their fans where to find their work, and they were followed around like stars. But here, in Charity, the boy was viewed as a vandal, a delinquent, a screw-up with a blur over his face. He'd bravely scaled the highest points in town and pasted them with exotic animals, and for this he got community service and a criminal record. This didn't seem right.

The giraffe and the hippo were scrubbed off first. Some of the high school students tried to save the gorilla. They linked arms and formed a human fence at the base of the water tower to keep the crews from climbing up to peel and wash away what their friend had done. This made Sara feel embarrassed all over again. Why were kids the only ones who saw the animals the way she saw them? Why did she see the animals the way kids saw the animals? She should've had a more mature response.

The students wouldn't budge. They planted themselves at the foot of the water tower for a day and a half until the cops showed up. Still they wouldn't go. Not until the Tasers.

Jake laughed. "Ouch."

"Three kids were Tased and you think that's funny?"

"They were in the way."

"What if it was one of your girls?"

"You've taught them better."

When she picked the girls up from school, she could tell that something was wrong with Bea. She was about to ask her what was the matter when Bea beat her to it.

"I made a hundred on my capital quiz and Berkeley made a 92 and called me a cheater just like my daddy."

"Don't listen to Berkeley."

"She's such a bitch."

Lizzy put her hands over her ears when she heard the word *bitch*.

"Don't talk like that."

"What kind of a name is that, anyway? Berkeley?"

"Better than what you called her."

"She deserves it."

"Nobody deserves it."

"A bitch is a female dog," Lizzy said.

As Sara drove the girls home she could see the water tower, cleaned and back to normal, a gorilla-less bubble above the tops of the pines.

Sara decided that an appropriately mature response was a letter to the editor of the paper. The *Charity Register* only came out twice a week so it was impossible to have written the letter in time to save the gorilla, but she went ahead with it anyway, practicing what she preached to the girls about follow-through. In it she wrote that the animals had been unique and original and funny, and while they may not have been the ideal images the town wanted to project to thousands of travelers cruising up and down I-75, the people had to admit that the animals made them smile. In the letter she had trouble coming up with the right word to use for *kids*. She didn't want to call them *kids*, or *boys and girls*, or *youth*. All of those words sounded vaguely condescending. So she settled on young adults. "Obviously the young adults of Charity want to feel like they are being seen and heard, like they have a place to express themselves. We should offer them a broad canvas instead of erasing their best efforts," she wrote. She was proud of this last line.

Jake said he liked the letter overall but that you couldn't really erase a canvas, so the metaphor wasn't exactly right.

"What do you mean?"

"You can erase pencil, but not paint, so it's more like you want to say rip up their fabric or mineral spirit their spirits. That's good. Something like that."

"I don't think so."

"Or you could say we should offer them a sheet of paper and a pencil instead of erasing their efforts."

"That's lame."

"You wrote it."

"What I wrote wasn't lame."

"I'm just saying."

In the letter she proposed turning the façade of the old movie theater into a public graffiti wall. The building was about four stories high, all brick, and used to house the one-screen movie theater back when people like Jake's parents were growing up. It had been closed for years. The south facing side of the building was painted with the chipping remains of an ancient ad for ice cold bottles of Coca-Cola. 5 cents. The town could paint over it, give all their citizens a free white wall to do as they saw fit. The Water Tower Zoologist could paste his animals. Kids could spray paint their names in neon letters. They could draw cartoons. The park district could project movies on the wall on summer nights. The wall would be a living and breathing piece of art representative of Charity and its people.

They didn't run her letter to the editor. She got an email response back thanking her and apologizing that *The Register* didn't have room for all the excellent letters they received. This was obviously part of a form letter, but at the end were a few lines that addressed her concern directly. *Graffiti is used to communicate gang territory. Do you really want that as a representation of Charity?*

"This is crap," she told Jake. "There are no gangs here."

"They're called something different," he said.

Sara offered Lo two hundred and fifty dollars to go to the hardware store, buy her some white exterior paint, some rough nap rollers and some extenders, then to drive one of the company's cherry pickers to the old movie theater in the middle of the night and lift her up and down in the bucket while she painted the south wall white. As far as she knew Lo was legal.

"It'll take too long," he said. "A brick is a sponge. You'll never finish. Tell you what. Double it and we'll do it for you."

This was a lot more money than she wanted to spend to prove a point, but she agreed and paid him in cash after he went with her to the ATM.

He didn't tell her when they'd do it, but he promised that it would be done by the end of the week.

She drove by the old movie theater every day to take the girls to school, even though it was out of the way.

On Monday nothing had changed.

On Tuesday nothing had changed.

On Wednesday nothing had changed.

On Thursday nothing had changed.

She figured Lo had taken her five hundred dollars and spent it all on Corona Light and tamales. Now she hoped Lo was illegal. She'd turn him in.

But on Friday the job was done.

The entire south facing wall of the old Charity Theater was a stark and beautiful white, total white, except for thin shadows cut by power lines across the glossy, gleaming brick. Sara pulled over.

"What are we doing?" Bea asked.

"Do you have markers? Crayons? What's in your backpacks? Just grab your backpacks."

They all got out of the car and went to the wall, Lizzy and Bea with their backpacks and Sara with her morning travel mug full of sweetened coffee. She almost didn't want to touch it. It reminded her of the animals, the surprise way they'd appeared overnight, as if the giraffe and hippo had climbed the towers on their own to see what they could see, as if the gorilla had wanted to announce something to the whole town and found the highest point to deliver his message, as if they had all been alive once but were only able to move safely under cover of darkness, like something out of a storybook, and when day broke they were forced to slip back into one dimension, adhering themselves to the closest solid structure they could find.

Before long Lizzy had her markers out. She was scribbling in purple against the rough surface of the brick, lines, nothing more, just lines, wavy and without direction. Then she started at one end of the wall, the marker gripped in her fist like a handlebar, and pushed it all the way to the other end, one long thin purple line. Bea laughed at her sister, then grabbed the black marker from Lizzy's bag and started writing her name in cursive, small and delicate and careful. Sara picked up the red marker, then put it back for the blue, then the green. She uncapped it and stood there staring up at the wall.

Trash Days

JOKES

One night, Walt and LeAnne Cox sat on their couch in front of a muted TV. LeAnne read through briefs while Walt fooled around on his laptop.

"Would you care if I bought a sex doll?" he asked.

"Is that a type of tomato?" LeAnne said without looking up from her work. Recently, Walt had gotten into tomatoes.

He scooted next to her on the couch and showed her a website. It was rather tasteful considering the product, the design more suited to an upscale lingerie boutique than a place to buy sex dolls. He told her he'd been doing some research, that she would be shocked at how many places were out there to buy dolls, and that this site, this particular one he showed her, had come highly recommended.

"Highly recommended? From who?"

"Chat rooms. Discussion boards. Forums."

Sometimes Walt and LeAnne played like this. One of them would see how far they could take a joke before the other one cracked or cracked up. Once, Walt had claimed to suddenly have a huge passion for sailing, so LeAnne signed him up for lessons on Lake Michigan, subscribed him to *Good Old Boat* magazine, bought him navy blue shorts patterned with tiny white sailboats. He came back from the second lesson green-faced and asking for ginger ale. Another time, LeAnne had stood her ground in an argument claiming that Emilio Estevez was underrated as an actor—that he was, in fact, her favorite actor. LeAnne now owned every Emilio Estevez movie. Her favorite had to be *Maximum Overdrive*, where Emilio saves a truck stop from machines come-to-life. However, after watching many of these movies, LeAnne no longer believed Emilio Estevez was underrated as an actor, but she never told this to Walt.

Walt clicked around on the website until an image of a naked doll popped up in the middle of the screen. Something wasn't right with this doll. She looked too young, too pert, too hairless.

"Not my type," LeAnne said.

"She's the basic," Walt said. "You fix her up."

Buttons and palettes lined the outside of the screen: rainbows of hair color, of lip and eye shades, beige to blue blocks of skin tones, breasts broken down by sizes. A ruler ran the length of the doll's torso to stretch her to Amazonian heights or shrink her to petite. Ass shape: apple to absent. Earlobes: attached, detached, or elfin. Hip width, muscle mass, exotic pubic shaving patterns, all were there for you to click and choose your dream girl.

"Give her red hair," LeAnne said. LeAnne had always wanted red hair, mostly because she thought it would be cool to have the nickname "Red." Redheads could get away with anything. When she dyed it once in high school, she'd ended up looking like Ronald McDonald with his hair on fire. Nobody called her "Red."

Walt clicked on some buttons and wavy long red hair appeared on the doll's head. LeAnne told Walt to give her green eyes. "Make her taller," she said. He clicked on the top of the doll's head and stretched her a few inches. "Make her thinner," LeAnne said. "Not that thin." The doll on the screen took shape, but she lacked something—individuality, the imperfect curves and symmetries, freckles, scars, a birthmark that would make her look more real. LeAnne wanted to give her a tattoo, a nose piercing, mismatched feet, a broken nose, moles, but she'd already done enough. "Your turn," LeAnne said.

"You're doing fine," Walt said.

"She's not for me."

Walt changed her hair color to blonde and painted her nails and lips candy apple red.

"Are you designing a sports car?"

He made the doll's boobs huge.

LeAnne looked down at her own boobs. "I thought you liked my boobs."

Walt bronzed the doll's skin.

"Now you're being mean." LeAnne moved far away to the arm of the couch and picked up her briefs. Walt kept clicking, laughing every now and then, typing. LeAnne peeked over to try and see what kind of woman he was making, but from her angle the monitor was all glare.

CLOTHES

At the end of last summer, Walt lost his job. He and LeAnne had worked at the same law firm — Miller and Fleisch — for seven years, the length of their marriage, and they had been lucky enough to drive into the city together every day and get thirty or forty or sixty more minutes together, depending on traffic. They would take turns driving. They would listen to audio books, drink coffee out of aluminum travel mugs, read each other stories from the *Tribune*. Both would probably have said it was their favorite part of the day. But when he lost his job, Walt insisted he needed the car to run errands, to head to job interviews, to drive to the gym. LeAnne had agreed, but she wanted a new car, one for herself. Walt had said that probably wasn't the smartest purchase given the fact only one of them was now working. And the parking. Did she have any idea how much parking cost? So LeAnne reluctantly agreed to take the train from their suburban home all the way downtown to save money.

The train station was a ten minute walk away. For the first few weeks of his unemployment, Walt had gotten up like he was going with her, like they had both suddenly decided to take the train to work. He took a shower, shaved, put on a tie, walked out the door with her, all the way to the train station before kissing LeAnne goodbye and waving to her like she was headed off to another country. Soon, though, the distance he traveled with her grew shorter. He stopped at the end of the driveway. He stopped at the front steps. He stopped at the door. He stopped at the breakfast table and waved to her from the front bay window. He stopped getting out of bed. Along with the shrinking distance, his clothes deteriorated from ties to ratty T-shirts, to ripped jeans, to pajamas, to his favorite gray and black gym shorts.

One day in October, LeAnne came home from work and found Walt in his pajamas, sitting in the exact spot she'd left him that morning, at the breakfast table, looking out of the front window as if he'd been thinking about going outside all day long but couldn't quite get himself up for it.

"Have you been sitting there all day?" she asked.

Walt stood up and hugged her. "Day's not over," he said. Then he dressed in his favorite gym shorts and told her he was going to "shoot hoops" to clear his head.

CONTAINERS

Thursdays were trash days. Walt never remembered to take the trash bin to the curb for pickup, so it was strange for LeAnne to see the bin already out. Her husband was still in bed when she told him goodbye and walked out the front door, figuring, because it was Thursday, she'd have to drag the bin to the end of the driveway herself. But there it was. She assumed Walt pulled it out last night when she hadn't been paying attention.

As LeAnne passed by the green bin, she noticed that the lid wasn't shut all the way. Some kind of long board propped the lid up at an angle like the hood of a car. She wondered what Walt was throwing away, so she lifted the lid. More boards, broken up planks, splintered and shattered blond wood that looked to LeAnne like pieces of a shipping crate.

She glanced back up to the house to see if Walt had gotten out of bed, if he was blowing across the top of his coffee mug while he stood at the bay window watching her. She wasn't trying to spy on him. Something odd was poking out of the trash and she simply wanted to know what it was, so she dug in. Some of the boards appeared to have been meticulously sawed apart, while some with jagged edges seemed blasted by a karate kick or broken over an angry knee. She inspected all sides of the wood for signs of what might have been delivered in a big wooden crate—what might have been delivered in a big wooden crate that Walt was obviously trying to hide from her by taking great pains to hack the evidence to pieces and by miraculously remembering to pull the trash bin to the curb. LeAnne couldn't find any markings on the wood—no burned-in logos, no packing slip, no mailing address, no invoice—but the lack of information only made her suspicion even stronger. You would probably send a sex doll unmarked. You would have to send a sex doll in a box she'd fit in. You would send a sex doll in a big wooden crate.

LEFTOVERS

Back in November, Walt had said he was going to start a food blog and name it *urachef2*. He bought a new digital video camera because he said his blog was going to have a DIY angle, complete with instructional videos and high quality images of food prep, step-by-step. LeAnne wanted to indulge him. He'd worked hard. He'd been fired under dubious circumstances, a political power play involving one dickhead equity partner. They'd saved enough money for a safety net. He was good at his job. He'd find work again. What harm could there be in letting him have a little fun? Go ahead and start a food blog, she thought. Knock yourself out. However, she did have to tell him the name for his blog sounded like a dictator. He told her she was pronouncing it wrong.

The camera wasn't the only item Walt bought. He bought expensive Japanese knives, a heavy mixer with meat-grinding and pasta-making attachments, silicone covered utensils — tongs, spatulas, brushes. LeAnne had no idea so many kitchen utensils came covered in silicone; she didn't even know what some of them were used for. He was going to teach people how to make their own ravioli, gnocchi, and spaghetti, how to grind their own meat and squeeze it into casings for sausages, and people would use his website because they could see the videos, pause them, copy his technique and instruction. Once he had a loyal social media following, he'd get sponsors and advertisements, and the money would flow in.

The whole idea worked out nicely as far as the food he prepared. They ate well, but after gourmet Thanksgiving and Christmas feasts, his efforts in the kitchen slowed down to once or twice a week, and LeAnne never saw a recipe, an image, or an instructional video on *urachef2*, just a placeholder on the website with a picture of carrots crossed like swords and the words "Coming Soon" arched in Comic Sans.

WORK

All day at work Leanne couldn't stop thinking about what she'd seen in the trash. She wanted to believe that the crate was for something else he'd ordered, that the doll had been, and still was, a joke. But if not, that meant Walt was hiding the doll from her, that he'd become the type of man who wanted—or worse, needed—a sex doll, and what kind of man was that? LeAnne knew all the stories. She'd seen all the movies. Emotionally disturbed men falling for inanimate objects of their own creation was a familiar tale. Lonely, deranged men fell for dolls, for statues, for mannequins, for little boy puppets come to life, their noses growing like erections. But Walt wasn't emotionally disturbed, lonely, or deranged—just unemployed.

LeAnne considered Googling "sex dolls" to see if she could find the website Walt had shown her last week but didn't think that was wise to do on her work machine. She checked their bank account. No out of the ordinary purchases for perverted products. She worked on a motion as best she could, but she couldn't take it anymore. She shut her door and called Walt.

"Did you actually buy her?" she asked.

"What?"

"Were you serious? Did you buy a sex doll?"

Walt cleared his throat. "Hold on," he said.

LeAnne heard him set the phone down. Then she heard what sounded like talking and laughter, a loud thud, something heavy hitting the floor. Maybe. She pictured him dragging a naked redheaded doll by the hair and tossing her in the hall closet, talking to her and laughing about his crazy, suspicious wife. *"My wife's on to us, Red. Quick, hide in the closet!"*

Walt got back on the phone. "What now?" he asked.

"Stop it."

"Oh, the doll. Yes. Her name's Tiffani."

"Tiffany?"

"Yes, Tiffani. With an *i*, not a *y*."

"How did you know I'd spell it with a *y*?"

"I know you."

He was right. She would spell it with a *y*. Only pole dancers would spell it with an *i*, pole dancers and sex dolls. LeAnne hated that he knew her that well.

"So you did buy her?"

"Is that a problem?"

From her desk, squeezed between the taller buildings on either side of her window, LeAnne could see a tiny slice of blue horizon—or gray, or green, or brown—that was Lake Michigan. Today it was pale blue, almost matching the sky. LeAnne liked that she could see that sliver of lake from her window. It had the ability to make the whole city feel less crowded. She had been looking at it a lot today.

"I don't believe you," she said.

"You shouldn't."

"Why would you buy a sex doll?"

"Good question."

"So what was in the crate?"

"What crate?"

"The crate in the trash."

"Why are you going through our trash?"

"Why are you hiding crates?"

Walt laughed. "Were you looking for your lost sense of humor?"

"Shut up."

"I bought some more equipment, lights and stuff. Next time I'll send you a purchase order."

It was money they didn't need to spend, but it was better than a sex doll. "You almost had me," LeAnne said.

"Almost?" Walt asked.

"Pretty good," LeAnne said. "Tiffani. With an *i*."

DREAMS

When LeAnne and Walt first started dating, they'd talked about their dreams, dreams of what they'd do if they weren't in law school. He'd said what he really wanted was to be a high school basketball coach, but the pay and lack of cachet wasn't worth it. LeAnne had said her dream was to be a lawyer.

"Nobody dreams of being a lawyer," he'd told her.

"I do," she'd said. And she wasn't lying. She'd never wanted to be anything else.

After Walt's interest in his food blog waned, he started going to high school basketball games. He became a fanatic. He talked to her about certain players, prospects from all over the Chicagoland area, their sick moves, what was special about their low post game, their ball-handling skills, which colleges were recruiting them. LeAnne thought all this was positive. She was not opposed to him working as a basketball coach if that's what he wanted to do; after all, it had been his dream. In January, Walt said someone named Coach Dee from a junior high school she'd never heard of had asked Walt to help out. Good. Maybe that was the first step.

Walt spent hours on his laptop, drawing up plays, researching opponents, chatting late at night with Coach Dee about strategy. At least that's what she thought, what she presumed. One night in bed he showed his project to LeAnne, what he'd been working on so hard. He slipped his headphones off and hooked them around his neck, yanked the plug out of the laptop and turned up the volume so LeAnne could hear. It was a video, a music video. One freakishly tall kid, number twenty-three, dunked over smaller boys, dribbled his way through packs of uncoordinated defenders, blocked lame shots, laughed, high-fived, and danced, all to a thumping hip-hop soundtrack. When it was finally over, LeAnne told Walt she thought it looked great and that she was happy he was getting some use out of his camera.

"I think I might submit it to a festival," he said.

"You don't have the rights to the music," she said.

"I was kidding," he said.

Coach Dee invited them to the team banquet. Walt asked LeAnne to come because the coach was going to show all of Walt's highlight videos. He wanted her to see them. He claimed they'd gotten better after the first one. When they got there, Walt's videos played silently in loops on flat screens set up on media carts. They weren't nearly as effective without the music, and people barely paid any attention to them.

MAGAZINES

LeAnne did not think about the doll again, did not think about the imaginary Tiffani with an *i*, until she and Walt had sex on Saturday night like usual. They both believed keeping a schedule was better than not having sex at all, but nothing was usual about this Saturday night. Walt did not feel like himself. His moves were unfamiliar and strange, like he'd learned something new from a men's magazine or pay-per-view and was itching to try it out. He left the lights on. He took all his clothes off before getting in the bed and roughly yanked LeAnne's T-shirt and underwear off without so much as a kiss. When he touched her, his hands felt like someone else's hands. His fingers twisted her nipples like they were tightening a screw. He squeezed her wrists and forced them against the mattress so hard she felt buried. She wanted to move, but her mind was not talking to her body, as if all her nerves had fizzled out, playing dead in defense. She figured he would stop, figured her lack of involvement would make him sit up in bed, ask her why she was just lying there, not moving. But the stranger in Walt's body kept going. He pulled her hair. He sucked on her neck. He bit her earlobe until she thought she felt blood and, finally, with a kicked heel into his thigh, yelled at him to get off.

Walt let go of her wrists and sat up on his knees. "What's the matter?" he asked.

"You're hurting me."

"What?"

LeAnne pinched her ear and stuck her knuckle in her mouth. She tasted metal. "I'm bleeding."

Walt stared down at her, his mouth open in confusion like she was making it all up. He swabbed a finger to her ear and showed it to her. No blood. He did it again. She saw nothing but his pale finger.

"You're being weird," he said, and rolled out of the bed. He flipped the light switch over his side of the bed and navigated to the bathroom in the dark.

LeAnne lay in the bed listening to the sounds in the bathroom, a cabinet opening and closing, the fan humming, and she wondered if Tiffani was in there, too, ready and unweird, doing whatever Walt wanted.

MONEY

In the thick of winter, when the snow had gotten too high, Walt bought a snow blower. In the morning he'd wake up and blow snow out of the driveway like he was getting ready to drive his car out of the garage. LeAnne saw this as another positive development, a sign that maybe he had an interview he needed to get to. He was clearing a path to go somewhere, to head out in a new direction. She liked the metaphoric possibilities of the clear driveway path. But a metaphor was all it turned out to be.

After each snow, he blew the driveway again, moved to the front walk and cleared it, then went next door and blew the neighbor's driveway without asking. Then he went farther down the street, blowing the sidewalk where it needed it, blowing more driveways when he saw a poor husband or wife struggling with a shovel. One of their neighbors paid him, and what made this gesture worse was that Walt took the money.

"You can't take money from our neighbors," she said.

"They gave it to me."

"They're your neighbors."

"I blew their driveway."

"You didn't have to."

"All the more reason to pay me."

LeAnne prayed for the snow to stop falling, but it kept up, every day it felt like, and so Walt kept it up too, blowing. She tried to tell herself it was great that he was keeping busy, that he had a task to work on, but she feared, because of the money, that maybe he was beginning to consider it his job. Whenever she saw Ellen at the drugstore or Mike Tolbert at the train station, she felt embarrassed, like she owed them something, like she'd stolen money from them. She tried not to make eye contact, glazing over, looking straight ahead, around them, through them, focusing stupidly on the newsstand or a bargain bin of hand sanitizer.

HAIR

The Monday after their bizarre Saturday night, LeAnne found four blonde hairs on the breakfast table as she bit into her English muffin. The hairs were lined up on the dark wood like lanes of traffic. LeAnne picked up the hairs and held the bundle to the daylight coming in from the window. They were all straight, all the same length, with a false sheen, too shiny. There was no way the hair was real, a real woman's hair. She blew on them, and the hairs waved in and out like tinsel. She wrapped them around her index finger and tried to yank them apart, but they wouldn't snap, too strong.

Walt grumbled out of the bedroom, poured himself a cup of coffee, and sat down with LeAnne. She stuck her hand under the table and let the hairs slip gently out of her fingers.

"What's on your agenda?" she asked.

Walt stared out the front window. "Thought I might plant an apple tree."

"Where do you hide her?"

"Hmm?"

"The doll. Tiffani with an *i*. Where do you hide her?"

Walt sighed and brought his mug to his lips. He blew across the surface, shooing steam off the top. "I'm not in the mood."

"She must always be."

He raised his mug to her in a mock toast to her humor.

"Can this stop?" she asked. "You're making me paranoid."

"What do you want me to say?"

"That she doesn't exist."

"She doesn't exist."

"Really?"

Walt sipped his coffee. "When did you stop taking jokes?"

LeAnne got up from the table and took her plate to the kitchen. Either he was lying about the doll, or LeAnne had something else on her hands. She shuffled all their friends and neighbors through her mind, trying to remember which ones hated their husbands, which ones Walt had ever called cute or flirted with at block parties, which ones had straight, strong, fake blonde hair.

ACCESSORIES

The neighborhood association contracted with a company named L&L Tow and Plow to plow their streets during the winter. In late February, after over two feet of snow fell in two days, Walt abandoned his blower and waved down Lawrence — the owner and presumed *L* in L&L Tow and Plow — and climbed aboard his plow. Walt and his video camera started riding with Lawrence on his rounds. On the days it snowed, Lawrence picked Walt up in the mornings and dropped him off at night.

Walt grew a salt and pepper beard that LeAnne actually ended up liking. It made him look distinguished, and he kept it trimmed and didn't let it grow out of control all down his neck. He looked older and ruggedly handsome. He started wearing blue jeans and heavy work boots, long-sleeved thermal underwear under flannel shirts. He'd never been that kind of guy, and even though she liked it, she felt like he was playing a part, like he wasn't really comfortable looking like that, the way he thought a guy who rides around in a plow all day should look. But he kept adding more and more to the character. He smelled of gasoline and oil and too long spent inside a truck. He brought home six-packs of cheap beer in cans, and he drank them one after the other out of foam koozies he'd bought from gas stations. He stuck his hand down his unbuttoned jeans while he

stations. He stuck his hand down his unbuttoned jeans while he watched extreme adventure shows on TV—shows where the host gets dropped into an inactive volcano and has to wit his way out, shows about fishermen, lumberjacks, people who blow up buildings for a living, build heavy machinery, haul tractor-trailers across icy roads.

In March a warm front came through, and with it, two days of rain that cleared a heavy winter's worth of snow. Patches still stood in shady areas of yards or in alleys shielded from the sun, but nothing was left to clear. Lawrence stopped coming by, and Walt put the snow blower in the garage for good. One morning when she was leaving for work, he came out of the bathroom, clean-shaven everywhere, head to toe, even his eyebrows. He looked like a missile wearing gray and black gym shorts. He told her spring had sprung and asked her if it was too early to plant tomatoes.

DIRT

She would have to catch him. Be it doll or neighborhood slut, Walt would not be stupid enough to entertain either one of them too close to when LeAnne got home from work. He wouldn't risk it. So the day after she found the hair, she walked to the train station, bought a pack of cigarettes, and waited. She hadn't smoked in two years, but she had two tall coffees and six cigarettes as she watched people board the morning trains for work. Every train that came by, she almost got on. She almost forgot it all and went to work, telling herself that his interest in whatever he was into would peter out like everything else, telling herself that she was overreacting, that he was going through a lot, and she should just let him be. But she had done enough of that.

LeAnne expected to have to get close to the house, to maybe sneak around to the backyard somehow. She wanted to assess the situation first, watch him before she guessed what he was up to. Perhaps he had coffee one day with Mary. She had straight blonde hair. Maybe he just needed someone else to talk to every now and then while she was at work. That would be okay. She'd thought of a ready-made excuse if nothing was going on. She had forgotten a binder. She thought it was at work, and when she got there she realized she'd left it at home and had to come all the way back to get it. Stupid LeAnne. She'd even remembered to bring home a binder last night, one with useless information, one she could intentionally leave. If Walt was there, sitting on the couch watching TV, no women or dolls anywhere, she'd walk right by him. "Forgot my goddamned binder," she'd say, pick it up, and try to believe he was up to nothing. But if she caught him ... LeAnne had thought more about not catching him than about what would happen if she did.

After two and a half hours, she left the train station and walked slowly back home. Once there, she stopped behind the arborvitae at the end of their driveway. She peeked around to see if Walt happened to be in the yard. She didn't see him, but she did see a woman. A blonde woman sat at their breakfast table in the front bay window. The woman wasn't moving—or didn't appear to be moving from where LeAnne stood behind the tree. LeAnne watched long enough to know the woman couldn't be real. No real woman could stay that still for that long. Walt approached the table with a newspaper. He popped open the newspaper and spread it out on the table. He looked out the window, and LeAnne snapped her head back. He couldn't have seen her there, but she waited. Ten seconds. Fifteen. Thirty. When she peeked again, Walt had pulled the curtain to cover half the window. The woman was no longer visible, but LeAnne could still see Walt. He had his video camera in his hand and was shooting whatever the woman was doing behind the curtain. LeAnne imagined her positioning herself in sexy and provocative poses. Walt stood on top of a chair and shot her from up high. He sank underneath the window frame for a low angle. He came outside and fixed the camera on a tripod to shoot through the window. He went inside and brought out, one-by-one, pieces of fruit, books, a hat, an umbrella, a board game. Then he left the camera on a tripod and went behind the curtain himself, disappeared for several minutes, where LeAnne's mind ran through a zillion carnal acts her husband was probably performing for the camera, but she did not move from behind the tree to stop him.

When he finally pulled the curtain, the woman was gone, and LeAnne wondered all over again what she'd seen, what she thought she'd seen. A blonde, motionless woman had been sitting at LeAnne's breakfast table. She knew it. She saw her. She did see her. Didn't she?

CLIPPINGS

LeAnne waited to make sure Walt's breathing was steady, an easy deep sleep rhythm, before she quietly got out of bed, picked his laptop off the floor, and went downstairs. Walt never password-protected anything. He claimed he had nothing to hide. She did not know exactly what to look for, but she didn't think his videos would be too hard to find. She was right. Walt had a folder titled *movs*, and inside that folder, smaller folders were neatly organized into a chronicle of his unemployment — everything he'd been into and slipped out of: *food, hoops, snow, tiff*. She clicked the folder named *tiff* and opened the first video she found.

Tiffani stood in the kitchen propped over a steaming tea kettle. The computer speakers let out a whistle, and LeAnne stopped the video. She went back upstairs and got Walt's headphones out of his bedside drawer. Seeing him asleep, she had second thoughts, like she shouldn't be doing what she was doing. She'd broken a trust. But Walt wasn't doing what he was supposed to be doing either. She went downstairs and plugged in the headphones. The clip was short. That's all there was to it:

Tiffani standing over a whistling tea kettle. She clicked another one. The doll was in the bathtub now, water running, covered to her neck in bubbles. LeAnne expected a naked Walt to come bouncing into the frame to bad porno music, but the clip ended with no action. The doll in the bathtub. Nothing more. The clips went on like this. Every one LeAnne opened, she saw just Tiffani, no one else: Tiffani holding a sucking vacuum cleaner, gripping an iron, readying to flip a piece of frying meat, washing dishes in yellow rubber gloves, snapping shears over shrubs; Tiffani in the bed with a sleep mask over her eyes; Tiffani by the curtains in the front bay window, staring out to the empty yard. And in every one of the clips, when LeAnne expected something to happen, to see Walt come on in and start to rip the girl's clothes off and have at her, the clip ended with Tiffani still dressed, still staring with her eyes wide and her mouth half-open like she was perpetually expecting something to happen, too. And for some reason, these images were worse, sicker than if she'd caught Walt videotaping himself using Tiffani for her intended purpose. That would've at least made sense.

Aside from her slight look of worry, mouth stupidly slack — easier to stick things in, LeAnne guessed — the doll was pretty. Tiffani was pretty. Her blonde hair was cut in a page boy style, and however Walt had managed to pick out her clothes, they were well-suited for her. She wore cute patterned sundresses, light and tasteful cardigans, knee-length skirts, scarves covering her hair, stylish black sunglasses. None of the clothes were

LeAnne's. In every clip Tiffani looked almost like the real thing. If it hadn't been for her open mouth, she might've passed for real. If someone had seen her from far away, they would have seen a real woman with real problems, problems like a real husband who dresses up a sex doll for fun.

LeAnne kept her eye on the stairs in case Walt happened to wake up. She'd say she left her computer at work. That she'd forgotten to send an important email. That she'd be right back to bed. No worries. She kept clicking clips, seeing the same images over and over—domestic Tiffani—until she found one that was different, a file labeled *romance2*. The clip started with blank, white snow, snow everywhere, then cut to other images: snow frosted over a fire hydrant, mailboxes, flakes falling through lamplight, footprints in the snow, a pyramid of snowballs, then cut to an image of their house shot from across the street on a winter's night. Light slipped from behind the curtain in the front bay window. It was the only light that was on. A loud scrape of a plow sounded off screen, and Lawrence's truck pushed swiftly and noisily through the frame left to right.

The image cut to their breakfast table, where Tiffani sat with the newspaper open, a coffee mug and a red apple next to her red fingernails. Again LeAnne thought she'd see Walt enter, but he didn't. The movie kept going on, locked on an immobile Tiffani, forever it seemed, until LeAnne noticed the apple was changing. She hadn't seen the cut, but the apple had a bite out of it, then a few seconds later, another bite. Everything else stayed still in the frame except for the invisible bites being taken from the apple, then a fade to black and a fade in to full morning sunshine, back outside, where Tiffani leaned on a snow shovel in an empty driveway. She was covered in a giant puffy coat and snow hat with pom-pom, mouth and neck wrapped in a scarf, but the yard was green, the street and driveway clear, the snow all gone. A truck drove by in the opposite direction, right to left—not Lawrence's this time, just a regular pickup—and the movie was over. LeAnne wasn't sure what kind of romance Walt intended with all this, but as far as she could interpret, Tiffani had magically freed the earth from winter.

PIZZA

LeAnne called in sick with the intention of sending Walt on errands so she could search the house for Tiffani, but everything LeAnne asked for, they already had. Sprite, chicken noodle soup, Tylenol Cold and Sinus. She thought she had him with a craving for cranberry juice, but Walt called Mary, who he said would have some because she drank cosmos. LeAnne wondered how he knew Mary's drinking habits. Mary was glad to help and told Walt to tell LeAnne to feel better. She told him he should go to the movies, but instead he rented one from the pay-per-view options on cable. She faked a nap, hoping Walt would voluntarily bring Tiffani out to play, but he rented a second movie and laughed too loudly after she had decided to actually sleep. Later in the day she said she felt better and wanted pizza from a place she knew didn't deliver to their neighborhood. "They'll deliver if you talk to the right driver," Walt said. "Ask for Stuckey." He was right. Within an hour, they had a hot mushroom and black olive pizza brought to their door. He stayed by her side the whole day like she was dying. When they went to bed that night, he told her it was nice to have her home.

DOLLS

On Thursday LeAnne woke up earlier than normal, the morning still dark, and dressed quietly for work behind the closed door of their closet. If Walt decided to get out of bed for some reason, she'd tell him she had to get to work early for a conference call with overseas clients and was just about to head out the door.

She went to the garage first. She did not know where Walt kept Tiffani, but since she had never accidentally run into her anywhere, the doll had to be outside. And LeAnne had a good guess where: the metal cabinet where they piled junk and tools and extra cleaning supplies. It was tall enough for a doll. As she stood in front of the cabinet, she noticed some of the gray metal shelves had been removed and were leaning against the side of the cabinet. LeAnne pulled the cabinet doors open. No Tiffani.

Because the shelves were removed, the inside did look like Walt had made room for her at some point, but now she was gone. LeAnne thought she heard, off in the distance, the sound of the garbage truck already moving through the neighborhood.

She had to hurry. She quickly looked around the rest of the garage before returning to the house. Excluding the garage, the cabinet had been her best guess. She had to check everywhere now without waking Walt. Downstairs she checked the laundry room, the kitchen, the half bathroom, all the closets, the backyard deck, under the deck, shining a flashlight into all its darkened corners. No Tiffani. She went upstairs and quietly checked the guest bedroom, under the bed—they needed to clean under there better—in the guest closet behind piles of clothes intended for the Salvation Army, then on to the master bedroom, in their closet between plastic dry cleaner bags and behind stacks of old board games, then, with the flashlight, under their bed, also dirty.

Walt flopped from his back to his stomach. "Feel better?" he mumbled into his pillow.

"Yep. Looking for shoes," she said and kissed him on his cheek.

LeAnne went back downstairs and searched in places she knew Tiffani couldn't even fit, as if she might be a genie able to turn to smoke at the slightest suspicion. She pulled out vegetable drawers from the fridge and lifted up sofa cushions. She searched inside the grill, behind liquor bottles, in empty shoeboxes and between the folds of blankets and towels. She looked through the desk in his office and the filing cabinets, where she found two drawers stuffed with women's clothes. She felt like she could throw up.

LeAnne sat on the edge of the sofa, out of breath, frazzled and frantic. The rumble of the garbage truck sounded closer. Again she doubted everything she'd seen, like she was the one going crazy, like she had never really seen the busted crate in the trash that day. Was it really blonde hair or pieces of plastic from a newspaper sleeve, thin strands of her own hair, graying? But there was no doubting the videos or those clothes. But what if the doll was someone else's doll? Lawrence's doll? A doll Walt borrowed because he had some crazy idea for a movie he wanted to make. Wasn't Teddy down the street laid off? He looked like the type of guy to buy a sex doll and not care who borrowed it. He and Walt could've been talking in the yard one day, talking about how they spent their time, about boredom and feelings of inadequacy, and Teddy could've just said, "You ought to think about getting a doll to screw. Passes the time. Borrow mine if you want a test drive." And Walt, wanting to make more videos, took him up on it, like asking a neighbor for cranberry juice.

That wouldn't make it any better.

The garbage truck was close, probably on their street. LeAnne went back to the garage, ready to start over, to retrace her steps. Maybe she hadn't looked hard enough. She reopened the gray metal cabinet.

Again, nothing in the cabinet. LeAnne opened the automatic garage door, knowing the sound might wake Walt but not caring anymore if it did. She'd tell him she was taking the car to work. Sometimes she drove on Wednesdays, but since she'd been sick yesterday, she would take the car today, so he could just deal with it. The car. She felt stupid for not putting it together in the first place. Of course. The car. She grabbed the keys from inside, hit the button on the remote, and popped open the trunk.

A trash bin banged against the garbage truck, probably at the Tolberts', the hydraulics crushing their leftover meat gristle, old sports magazines, plastic containers and bottles they refused to recycle.

LeAnne swallowed hard.

The doll crammed in the tight space looked too real, a real body, with those full wide eyes and that half-open mouth like she was gasping for air. Tiffani wore pajamas, a pair of silky Betty Boop pajamas. These were not LeAnne's. LeAnne turned around and saw the garbage truck pass slowly by the driveway. Their bin was not by the curb. She waved for the truck to wait, but the driver either didn't see her or didn't care. LeAnne shoveled her arms under Tiffani's arms and knees and pulled her out of the trunk. She was heavy, and her skin felt real—cool but real, with give and elasticity—not the plastic touch LeAnne imagined. Tiffani smelled like baby powder. LeAnne tried to turn and run for the truck, but Tiffani was too heavy, and she dropped her. Her body and head slapped on the floor, landing sprawled like she'd been tossed out a window. Her blonde hair, cut like a stage curtain, opened on her vacant and pleading face.

"Wait," LeAnne yelled to the garbage truck, but it was already two houses down, at Mary's, crushing up her empty nutrition bar wrappers and plastic sacks full of dirty cat litter.

LeAnne could put her back in the trunk, take her somewhere and bury her, dump her in a dumpster behind a greasy restaurant, leave her outside the high school for some boys to find for their best day ever. She looked down at Tiffani all crooked on the concrete slab. Her unbuttoned pajama top gaped open at her huge boobs. She had a tan line. Walt had bought her with a tan line. LeAnne stared at the light shift in color from tan to pale, as if the sun was something that could warm her skin. LeAnne knelt down next to her and buttoned up her pajamas. She stuck her finger in Tiffani's mouth. She had teeth and even a tongue. LeAnne pulled her rubbery tongue out and left it wedged in the corner of her open mouth like she'd been strangled, then dragged Tiffani by her blonde hair to the middle of the driveway. She had planned to wave down the garbage truck if it came back by, but when she saw the snow blower parked in the corner of the garage, she got a different idea.

She peered into its mouth and saw the corkscrew-looking blades. She fingered their edges. She looked out to the driveway, Tiffani flopped in her pajamas in the brightening morning. Tiffani would have to be smaller, much smaller. LeAnne couldn't just run over her face first with the blower and expect the paddle to keep on chugging, whirring her up and spitting

43

her out skull to toe. Bit by bit it would have to swallow her: hair, ears, nose, lips, fingers, hands, boobs, toes, her body disassembled then fed in the mouth of the machine. It would take time. Walt would catch her. He would hear the noise of the snow blower and get curious. She needed him to catch her. He would run downstairs and look out the front bay window, and there they'd be—Tiffani sliced to pieces, her head rolled in the yard like a basketball, fingers spread around like chopped carrots, a whole foot already shredded and blown to a silicone blizzard, and LeAnne leaning on the blower, staring back at him, her mouth open, breathing heavy from all her hard work.

Rapture

I first saw Mary at the live nativity auditions. She was barefoot, decked out in a motherly white robe and sky blue headscarf like she'd already gotten the role, while all the other girls were tarting around in short-shorts and deep cut V-neck sweaters and beat-up canvas sneakers, popping their chewing gum and taking selfies with their elbows akimbo. The audition didn't ask for much. I said who I wanted to be, and they asked me if I had arthritis or any lower extremity issues that would prevent me from staying on my feet for six hour shifts. Then they asked me to stand still for five minutes and stare at something in the room. I picked Mary. She was sitting down in a line of metal folding chairs, holding a baby doll in her arms and rocking it like it was the one true Messiah. I was flooded with peace and love.

"You're a shepherd," they told me.

"What about Joseph?"

"You're no Joseph," they said.

The gig was in the front yard of a mega church off I-75 south of Atlanta, a thirty minute drive from my apartment, forty-five to an hour in our notorious traffic, but I needed the work, which was why I signed on with a Christian talent agency in the first place. My sheep weren't real, but they were three-dimensional. Ceramic. Baby Jesus wasn't real either, but nobody seemed too bothered by this fact, probably because he was battery-operated, and his little arms and legs went around in circles as an attempt at authenticity, and if you stared at him long enough, his moves would begin to seem totally random and baby-like, almost as if he'd miraculously come alive under Mary's tender gaze.

It took me until the 21st of December to ask her out.

"We may have breakfast at eight o'clock," she said, like a queen granting me an audience.

Despite the early hour, I took the audience.

▼▼▼

If we both worked the evening shift, four to ten, me and Balthazar would meet at a bar back in East Atlanta for a few drinks. The night before my morning date with Mary was no exception. Balthazar was the first dude I'd ever seen order eggnog. It was last call. He said he was feeling adventurous.

"You reckon she's a virgin, Mary?" Balthazar asked, a line of nog-froth riding his upper lip.

"Doesn't make a difference to me."

"She's probably one of those that'll make you marry her first."

"I'll start with breakfast."

Balthazar huffed. "See," he said. "This is why I don't usually hang with the shepherds."

"I'm not a real shepherd," I said. "I do want a dog, though. A real smart one like shepherds have. Shepherds usually have real smart dogs."

Balthazar took another nip from his glass of holiday cheer. "Dogs are free at the goddamn humane society."

"Maybe I'll go get one."

"No, you won't." Balthazar made this retching sound like he was scratching the back of his throat before he hopped off the stool and ran into the bathroom.

He was in there for some time, so I went to check on him. I found him hovering over the sink, his cheeks wet and puffy, his fingertips drawing his eyelids down like he was trying to pop out a contact lens. "I think I'm allergic to eggs," he said. I offered to drive him to the emergency room, but he said he'd be all right.

As he backed his car out of his parking spot, I saw him load up and fire a sneeze into the steering column, causing him to surge the gas and crash his rear bumper into a white van. I knocked on his window. "I'll take you," I said.

He moved over to the passenger's side. "Good shepherd," he said.

He wheezed the whole way there, but once we got inside he seemed better, so Balthazar was deemed low priority among the late night knifings and drunken hijinks gone awry. We waited for hours, and after exhausting the magazine inventory,

I found a threesome of armless chairs that made for a nice place to curl up. I fell asleep, my jacket serving as a comforter.

When I woke up, Balthazar was gone. The triage nurse handed me a red envelope and told me my friend had left and didn't want to bother me because I looked so peaceful. Inside the envelope was a Christmas card, a manger scene on the front not unlike the one we depicted every day at the mega church, minus the faithful throngs praising our life-likeness. "Unto You A Child Is Born," it said. I opened the card and saw he'd scribbled a message for me. "No good way to deliver this news to you, bro, but I'm in love with Mary."

It took two slow-going buses to get me back to my car at the bar, at which point dawn was already breaking. I knew if I hauled ass I could probably make it to my date in time, but when I turned the ignition, I got nothing but clicks. I checked under the hood, which was already popped without me having to pop it. Balthazar was way ahead of me. The bastard had stolen my battery.

A forty-two dollar Uber ride later, I arrived at the Waffle House just in time to see Mary wheeling out of the parking lot in her blue Mazda. I knew it was hers because I recognized her bumper sticker from work: *In the Event of Rapture This Car Will Be Unoccupied*. I wasn't sold on the likelihood of the rapture or my inclusion in it, but I really hoped it didn't happen before I could get to the humane society.

▼▼▼

I didn't see Mary again until New Year's Eve, at a party the agency threw for all its actors. She walked up to me while I was digging my hand into a bowl of Chex mix.

"I thought you disappeared," she said.

I'd called in sick for the rest of my live nativity contract figuring they'd be all right with just two shepherds. "Sorry," I said. "Family emergency. I didn't have your number."

"Is everything okay?"

"I'm looking forward to a better year."

Mary grabbed a sandwich triangle from a red and green striped holiday plate and popped the whole thing in her mouth.

"Can I get you a drink?" I asked.

"I don't think there's any alcohol here," she mumbled through a mouthful of pimento cheese.

"Sure there is," I said.

She followed me out to my car where I had a fifth of Jack smuggled in the center console.

"You seen Balthazar?" I asked.

"He's gone. He got a part in one of those *Left Behind* movies."

"The end of the world ones?"

"That's correct."

"With Kirk Cameron?"

"I'm not sure he's in this one."

I twisted open the bottle and dropped the cap in a cup holder. "Are you two, like, a thing?"

"Me and Kirk Cameron?"

"No. Balthazar."

"Not that I know of."

I swigged from the bottle. "That's good."

"Are you born again?" she asked.

"I've been baptized, if that's what you're asking."

I passed her the Jack. "Every bit helps," she said. She stared at the open mouth of the bottle, held the liquid up to the street lights eyeing its enticing hue, then plucked the cap out of the cup holder and twisted it on tight without ever taking a drink. She put the Jack back in the console, and we talked for a little while. I found out that Mary's real name was Mary, and that she was younger than me, but not young enough as to make my desire criminal.

When it was close to midnight, we went inside for the countdown. Everyone was in good spirits, their faith renewed for the days ahead. And I knew what I would do once we counted down to one and everyone shouted, "Happy New Year!" And I knew from her smile that Mary knew what I was going to do and was saying *go ahead.* And when we kissed it was electric, sparklers and lightning and confetti and jet packs and Hawaii, and after we let go, we threw our arms around each other and sang that song nobody knows the words to but is all about forgetting your old, dead friends.

"You taste like booze," she said.

"I love you," I said.

"You don't even know me."

"You are the mother of God," I said.

Mary was a filthy housekeeper. Everything in her apartment was dirty—dirty dishes, dirty clothes, dirty food-smeared magazines, dirty dust bunnies carrying around other dust bunnies—and she had an entire wall full of crosses above her bed, which served to remind her of the sacrifice Christ made for her. Since she'd been born again, Mary had been tempted many times to backslide, although attentive prayer, the right social group, and the Christian talent agency had helped her keep her faith. She told me she would "prefer" not to have sex again before she was married, but I convinced her there was a threat of icy road conditions, especially on bridges and overpasses, so she caved and said I could stay in her bed. We kissed and did some other things that usually lead to more things, but she stopped herself and put her head on my chest muttering her multiplication tables, "Two times one is two. Two times two is four. Two times three is six. Two times four is eight." I fell asleep before she got to her nines.

Sometime in the middle of the night I woke up when I felt a bug scurry across my cheek. I got up and checked under the kitchen sink where most people who clean things keep their supplies. A quarter bottle of Windex lurked at the back behind a calcified shaker of Comet. First I picked up all the junk and sorted what didn't look like trash into neat piles that I placed on an ottoman ripped to shreds from what must've been a former cat, because there was no cat to be found. I carried around her small plastic trash can from the kitchen and stuffed it full. Once I could see most of the surfaces, I went after them with the Windex. Before then, I had no idea a woman's habitat could be so disgusting. I left the dishes piled in the sink because I didn't want the noise to wake her up, but I did fill it up with hot water and suds to try to soak off all the crud.

She woke up anyway and stood against the doorframe to the kitchen in a T-shirt that hung off her shoulder and struggled at the hem to make it to mid-thigh, her arms folded across her chest.

"I thought you left," she said.

I shook my head. "Just cleaning."

"I'm a mess."

"We're all sinners."

"Do you give back rubs, too?"

I thought she was going to lie down on her stomach in the bed so I could massage her naked back and shoulders, hopefully with some kind of sensual lubricant, but that wasn't the kind of back rub she was talking about. She wanted me just to hold her and run my fingers lightly up and down her back, under her T-shirt, while she rested her head on my chest. Her hair smelled like candy canes and buttermilk. Something was wrong with her spine, the knobs uneven and crooked, and every time I touched a certain spot, she shuddered. I asked her if that's where her wings had been.

"Don't ruin this," she said.

Mary went with me to the humane society to get a dog. He was a mutt, smallish, brown and black with some white on the tips of his pointy ears. I named him Chris, because I like it when pets have people names. Chris and Mary hit it off right away. He ran to her and she bent down to greet him and he licked her face and she scratched behind his ear. She even got him to sit for a dried up piece of granola bar she found in her purse. Having a dog was a challenge, but he filled my days with a joyful purpose, made me beholden to a creature other than myself, and I began to understand the long and storied historical relationship between man and canine, best friends indeed.

I got a commercial gig for a weekend in St. Simons, where I played a counselor at a Christian youth camp. I held an earnest heart-to-heart with a young boy while we sat on a piece of driftwood near the surf. No audio. We moved our lips but didn't say anything. Mary took care of Chris at her place while I was gone, and when I came back, he didn't want to leave. When I tried to drag him out by his collar, he hunkered down and growled at me, something he'd never done before. When I threw a treat out the door hoping he'd fetch it, he sat on her rug and blinked his heavy dog lids at me—*you think I'm an idiot?*

Mary was no help. "He likes it here," she said.

Probably because food hid under every paper towel, between the couch cushions, under the bed, in corners and closets, dog paradise. Pretty soon Chris made a full migration over to her place, which was okay because it gave me plenty of pretense to stay over. The three of us would sleep in the bed together, Chris between us, serving as a buffer. But whenever I got home and saw his empty kibble dish, his leash hanging by the door, his rubber chew bone unchewed, it was like he'd run away, or like I was some crazy person holding on to empty symbols of my dog's life long after he'd died.

I told Mary I needed my dog back.

"Chris is *our* dog," she said.

Then she told me it was time to meet her parents.

They lived in a modest ranch house in a small town near Macon. Their house was clean, so there was no telling where Mary'd gotten her lazy housekeeping. Her mom wore an apron that said "Goose the Cook" while she made us grilled pork chops, asparagus, and mashed potatoes. Chris tromped around the back yard, chewed on sticks, treed squirrels, having a grand time. Mary had warned me that her dad was an alcoholic, but she'd said that just meant he was in bed by eight o'clock. She had two older brothers, but neither one of them lived there anymore. After supper we sat in their family room and her parents showed me pictures of Mary when she was little.

"Mary has always been an actor," her mom said.

"A drama queen," her dad said.

We watched a video of Mary when she was in seventh grade. She was in a play called *The Best Christmas Pageant Ever*, and she played this urchin named Imogene Herdman who smoked cigars and cursed in church and was the ringleader of the Herdman crew, all of them trouble. Imogene bullies her way into playing Mary in the church pageant where she undergoes a transformation and demonstrates to everyone the true meaning of Christmas. Mary had played Mary before. She was cute in this play and superior to everyone in it, and Mary in the room smiled at the compliments we were giving Mary on the TV, but as the play went on, her dad's compliments turned bitter. He clapped at times when clapping wasn't called for and laughed an obnoxious, knee-slapping guffaw at lines of hers that weren't funny, climaxing in a series of insincere *Bravos!*

"Genius!" he said, his hands slowly clapping. "A child prodigy! Steve, are you bearing witness to her gift?"

My name's not Steve, but I kept my mouth shut.

Mary tried to get up and walk out of the room, but he jumped from his chair, sloshing his vodka across the carpet, and grabbed her by the elbow.

"Imogene and her pussy willows," he said. "Always bullying boys with pussy willows. She get you that way, Steve?"

I didn't fully sense what was happening, but I knew he was upsetting Mary, and that upset me.

"No, sir," I said and stood up. "I think you should apologize."

"Why don't you go fuck yourself."

I'd never seen anything like this in real life. Behavior of this sort was not on display in my household, a generally loving and nurturing one. Probably what made me who I am today, for better or for worse. "You can say whatever you want to me, but tell Mary you're sorry."

Her mom looked down into her drink and would not look up, staring at it the way she must've done every night for the entirety of her marriage. Her dad nodded his head. Mary cried. He cupped his free hand around the back of Mary's neck and pulled her to his face and kissed her hard on the lips before wheeling around to face me, wobbling as he spun. He smiled, took a dramatic bow, and stumbled off to his bedroom, almost knocking over a side table along the way.

He never did apologize.

We got ready for bed in a bathroom at the end of a long hallway. Mary wore nothing but that loose T-shirt and her underwear. She pushed her hair back with a headband and washed her face with some pre-moistened sheets, flossed and brushed her teeth. My pee smelled like asparagus. She closed her eyes and held her nose. I washed my face and brushed my teeth, following her lead.

"Thank you," she said. She kissed me, and given the emotional thrust of the night, things got heated pretty quickly and were headed in a direction she'd "prefer" not to head, but she didn't break into her multiplication tables, so the situation was allowed to escalate. I was on top of the toilet lid, shirt off, boxers still on, Mary straddling me, and I told her to wait. I said we ought to wait until we got married like she'd said she wanted to wait.

"Are we getting married?" she asked.

"You want to?"

She got off me. "All right," she said, "but you'll have to ask my daddy."

"I don't think he likes me," I said.

"He won't remember a thing," she said.

Mary and I couldn't sleep in the same bed under her parents' roof, so I was sent to a twin bed in one of her brother's rooms, while she and Chris went off together. My bed had a footboard that came up short. Gold trophies were all over the shelves. Medals hung off the closet knobs. This brother of hers was a runner, or at least sometimes he was a runner, other times he was a wrestler. On top of his desk, where he used to sit and do homework and dream of wrestling glory, was a globe, an electric globe plugged into the wall with a white cord and a thumb wheel switch. I got out of bed and clicked the switch to see what this was all about, and not only did it glow cool and blue from the inside, it spun slowly on its axis with a minimal hum. I watched the globe spin for a while, high from all that had happened. I watched the globe, and I noticed there were countries on there that didn't even exist anymore, countries lost to history, places I'd never be able to take her.

I didn't ask her dad the next morning, because I never saw him again. Her mom made us a big breakfast of eggs and sausage and toast and fresh squeezed juice and told us that Mary's dad wasn't feeling well. Mary didn't even tell him goodbye before we drove home. I can't say I blame her.

We never did get married, even though I'm pretty sure I was in love with her, and I know I would've gone through with it had her dad been sober enough to deliver his blessing. I like to remember her at the live nativity scene. That battery-operated, fake baby Jesus coming to life before her. I'd imagined our whole future then, Christmas after Christmas after Christmas, the two of us telling our kids how God was born the night we'd met in a manger. We had two more good months before Balthazar rolled back into town and whisked Mary off to some promised stardom in California. She left Chris behind. I was glad to have him, but I could tell how much he missed her by the way he chewed up one of my throw pillows and spread the contents of my garbage all over the kitchen, leaving another mess for me to pick up.

Nesting

After Megan's first trip to the doctor at six weeks, Tate felt the urge to build something, so he went to The Home Depot and ordered a backyard playset. His own dad had been one of those dads who could build anything, take scrap metal and build a custom-made smoker, take some popsicle sticks and build a scale model White House. If a wall didn't have a window, and he wanted a window, he could make a window. He'd done all this when Tate was little, but Tate hadn't inherited these necessary dad skills. What he needed were ready-made parts and easy assembly instructions, all available at The Home Depot.

The playset he ordered was modeled after a giant ship, and it was awesome—way too expensive—but awesome, exposed from the stern so you could see all the multiple levels, hammocks swinging in the hold, portholes offering fictional ocean views. A swingset hung off the starboard side, and a large deck sat atop the ship with a free-spinning steering wheel, a mast with ascending rope ladders, a plank for sending mutineers to the sandbox below, and a crow's nest to watch out for neighborhood marauders coming to steal your treasures. Fake barnacles even stuck to the hull for gripping and climbing. It looked dangerous, but a little danger was good. Life was fragile. A kid should learn this lesson early.

On a cold Saturday morning, two guys in a semi-truck delivered the playset. Once unpacked and splayed out in the yard, the unassembled parts looked like an excavated shipwreck, like Tate had dug deep into a sea bed and unearthed some long lost schooner. The instructions came in a booklet, and before he even read them he knew he was in over his head. The drawings were clear enough, complete with faceless cartoon characters easily putting the ship together piece by piece, but after five hours of freezing his ass off he had nothing standing but the broad hull of the ship and a wobbly swingset. Nothing was sturdy. The ship swayed like it might capsize from a strong breath or the accidental whip of a squirrel's tail. He knew he'd messed something up, left some parts out or attached a random flange or bracket in the wrong place, but it was anybody's guess how.

Megan had been gone all afternoon raiding one of her friend's closets for maternity clothes. He hadn't told her what he'd done. He'd wanted the ship to be a surprise. It was. When she saw what was happening in the backyard, she got pissed. She told him this was a sure jinx and yelled at him for building a playground for their corn kernel. She went inside in tears.

Tate felt like a failure. The instructions were clear and easy, giant fucking numbers and letters, and each illustrated square told him the tools and parts he needed for that step, but somehow he'd managed to screw the whole ship up and make his wife cry all at the same time. Well done.

He gave up, grabbed a beer out of the fridge, and took it with him to the shower.

When he came out he felt better, warm and loose. He dried off and put on pajama bottoms and a T-shirt. He still had Sunday, a new day with new possibilities and a new clear eye for the job. He'd tackle it tomorrow.

Megan was propped up in the bed reading one of her pregnancy books. They'd originally planned to wait a while before starting a family. Megan wasn't totally sold on having kids at all. This was an accident, so now she was educating herself. She'd bought a million books on pregnancy and how to have a baby and what to buy for the baby and how to care for the baby once it popped out. Why weren't her books a jinx?

"You're nesting," she told him. She shook the book at him. "Parents-to-be will get this need to fix stuff up before the kid comes. It's biological. Like a bird."

Tate sat on the bed next to her and put his hand on her belly. Nothing much was happening, only under the surface. The doctor had told Megan her embryo was the size of a corn kernel. Tate thought it was weird that her doctor called it an embryo.

"What kind of bird?" he asked.

Megan looked up from her book, the skin around her eyes still puffy and red from crying. "An odd one."

"Eagle?"

Megan smiled and shook her head.

"I can be an eagle," he said.

Twelve and a half weeks must've been the jinx-free date in all her books because that's when they finally got to tell everyone. Once they shared the news, sent the emails and text messages and made the phone calls to the most important people, the well-wishes and unwanted advice poured in. Megan's parents said this was exactly what they'd hoped for when they'd helped buy them a house—grandkids!—and suggested Tate and Megan start saving money "ASAP" because the "little treasure" would be "off to college in no time." Tate's mom said, "Thank you, Jesus," and told him that his dad was smiling "from a fishing pond up in heaven." Tate's oldest brother warned him that Megan was going to go "bat shit crazy," that she'd have unexplainable crying fits, that she'd develop bizarre cravings, and that he would not have sex for a "very, very, very, very long time." His other brother asked him if he was sure the kid was his. "You never know," his brother said. "You think you know, but you never *know*." Tate figured both his brothers were just trying to scare him.

Tate worked as a legal assistant at a mid-size law firm downtown while he procrastinated on making a decision about going to law school. Megan liked to tease him about being a secretary. She was between teaching jobs, and now Tate worried she might never go back to work, a move that might necessitate law school and its potential higher earning power. He didn't think of himself as a secretary. He liked the work because the pay was pretty good and he got to be around the law without practicing law, without indenturing himself to the firm and to billable hours. Leaving the place at a decent hour, at home in time for a few beers, dinner and TV, or a night out with friends, made him feel like he was his own man.

At work Dana came into his cube and hit him on the shoulder. "You dirty dog," she said. "I have to find out in the break room from Zoe." Tate wondered what other gossip Zoe spread about him in the break room while she was vending out her Flamin' Hot Cheetos. Dana bent over and hugged him in his office chair, squeezing him tightly. She lingered on the hug, slowly rubbing his back, her ozone-scented hair tickling his nose.

Something was different about Dana today. Dana was hot. She'd never been hot before. Weird, yes. Hot, no. Dana was older than Tate, 40s maybe? He couldn't tell exactly, but he'd never thought much about her life outside the law firm, especially after that depressing Halloween party last year. She was always just Dana, kind of his boss, the quirky partner with a pert spray-do and a closet full of patterned pant suits. She did have nice arms, though—from yoga, she said. She always made a point of taking her jacket off to reveal her muscular arms, no matter the weather. But she was a weirdo, artsy-craftsy, not your typical lawyer at all—if there was such a thing. She made her own decoupage posters from magazine cutouts and postcards that she put in expensive frames and hung in her office. She knitted. He mostly felt sorry for her. But today— today she was hot. Maybe it was because Tate's wife had already taken to wearing elastic waistband jeans and loose-fitting dresses that looked like California king size sheets, had steadily been complaining about how bad she felt, in the morning, at night, all the time. She wasn't even showing.

"Did you …? Is there something different?" Tate asked.

She nodded. Her hair stayed put. "I met someone," she said.

That explained it. She'd met someone. She had the warm honeyed glow of having met someone, someone she'd probably had sex with within the last twenty-four hours. He could tell. On some women you could just tell. He thought he could tell with Dana, partly because she never looked like this before, like a lighthouse.

She told Tate she'd met this guy at a craft fair. His name was Stan. Dana's newest sad craft was making felt puppets of famous people, incredible likenesses of old rock stars like Elvis and James Brown and screen legends like Clark Gable, and she sold this goofy shit at craft fairs. Obviously not for the money.

She also made small puppet key chains in the shapes of animals. Where did she find the time? Tate had one on his own set of keys, a small, round, brown and tan monkey face.

"What's his craft?" Tate asked.

"Stan's an out of work union electrician," she said.

How weirdly specific. "Does he light up your life?"

Dana posed like she was holding a light bulb over her head. "Can't you tell?"

Tate never got around to finishing what he started. The pieces of the playset sat in the yard for weeks, gathering a yellow layer of spring pollen and fallen blooms. He kept promising himself and Megan that he'd do it, that this would be the day, but this was never the day. Then he came home on a Friday after a long week and it was done. He'd just changed out of his work clothes and was washing his hands in the kitchen when he looked out the window above the sink and saw it in their backyard, a ship rising from the earth. He yelled Megan's name, but she didn't answer, so he went outside and checked it out. Awesome, as promised. Strong and sturdy. Solid. This ship wasn't going anywhere. He used the barnacles to hoist himself up to the top deck where he spun the steering wheel. He walked the plank and stepped off into the sandbox, leaving two deep footprints. The kid was going to love it, a ship, voyage-bound for anywhere he could dream.

Back inside, Tate found Megan sitting at the kitchen counter reading another one of her pregnancy books. Where had she been when he called her name? "Did you know there's actually no real scientific proof that breastfeeding is better for your kid?" Megan asked.

Tate wondered if she even knew about the ship, if some benevolent carpenter had seen the desperate wreckage and decided to lend a helping hand. Maybe she'd called The Home Depot and rented a guy. They probably did stuff like that. Rent-a-guy. "Who fixed the ship?"

"Think about it," she said. "Who breastfeeds?"

Tate figured most women breastfed their babies, if they cared about their babies. "Everybody."

"No. Middle and upper class women. So middle and upper class women probably will already have healthier and smarter babies because of other socio-economic advantages, not just because they breastfeed. It's correlation, not causality."

"Did you know the ship was up?"

"Yes," she said. "Your dad helped me."

Tate laughed and felt her forehead.

She jerked away from him. "I'm not joking," she said. "He talked to me like Obi-Wan Kenobi, except he sounded like Johnny Cash and not Alec Guinness."

Funny. His dad had kind of sounded like Johnny Cash. She had never met his dad. Tate grabbed a beer out of the fridge. "Seriously. Who fixed it?"

"Seriously. I fixed it. Your dad talked me through it. Told me what to do. Put this part here. Put that part there. He said I had a gift."

Megan was a deep believer in all things supernatural: ghosts, curses, psychics, aliens, jinxes. It was one of the reasons he loved her, her imagination. But she'd never claimed to be able to speak to the dead. This was new. His brothers would probably tell him it had something to do with hormones. Later he'd check all her pregnancy books under "paranormal delusions."

For now he could humor her. She wasn't crying, and she looked calm and relaxed for the first time in a long time. And the ship had gotten built. More than he could do. Tate sipped his beer and looked out the window again. He imagined playing out there with his kid, heeding orders to swab the deck, assuring his frightened toddler that it was safe to climb to the crow's nest, pretending to walk the plank and plummet to the sharks. He couldn't wait.

"So you're not breastfeeding?" he asked.

"I haven't decided."

"I'm pretty sure it's better for the kid."

"Not according to this." Megan closed the book and held up the cover. *Your Body, Your Body, Your Breasts*.

"Like The Who song?" Tate asked.

She looked at the cover, hummed the melody. "Never thought about it."

This was all new to Tate. He assumed that his wife would do what she could to give their baby the best opportunity to be healthy. This included breastfeeding. Plus, breastfeeding was a lot less expensive than formula. Why was this even a choice? "I think you should give it a shot."

Megan quickly closed the book and stood up. She walked over to where Tate was leaning against the counter and lifted his white undershirt, pulling it up and over his head and arms, quickly, so that he had to set his beer down to keep from spilling. She stuck her lips on his nipple and sucked, sucked hard and wet and slobbery. Then she bit him.

"Twelve times a day," she said. "Hours at a time. Until I'm raw and cracked and bleeding."

Tate wasn't sure what she was complaining about. It hadn't felt that bad.

▼▼▼

After weeks of Dana talking about Stan this and Stan that and generally becoming more and more attractive by the day—she'd done something new to her hair, less spray-and-hold, more relaxed, and she'd worn tight jeans to work on days other than Friday—Tate finally met the guy. He ran into them at one of his favorite lunch spots, Burgatory (*Burgers Just Shy of Heaven!*). Dana liked their veggie burgers, extra pickles. She was sitting at a table with this husky bald guy, both of them drinking milkshakes, hers chocolate, his strawberry. When she saw Tate come in, she grabbed him and dragged him over to their table. The guy was one of those heavy-set slobs who get lucky and land the pretty girl on TV sitcoms. The tight bands of his white golf shirt squeezed his hairy arms.

Dana introduced Tate. "This is my BFAW," she said.

Stan's puzzled look said he didn't get it either.

"Best Friend At Work," Dana said.

Tate was surprised to learn he was Dana's BFAW, but flattered, and glad she hadn't called him her secretary.

He went to the counter and ordered a cheeseburger, then changed it to a double with bacon and the works. He'd planned to take it all back to the office, but she insisted he stay and eat with them. When he joined them at the table, Tate noticed Stan had a pile of keys in front of him like he was the super of some building, a janitor at a skyscraper. The nest of keys was filled with feathers and jingle bells and all kinds of baubles and trinkets, including one of Dana's keychain animals: a rhino. Tate wondered if she gave people the animals she thought they resembled or deserved. Tate was a monkey. Stan was a rhino. Why did this rhino have so many keys?

Dana said that last weekend she and Stan had driven all over the state looking for antiques. This was a shared love of theirs: "antiquing." At her request, Tate grudgingly narrated his weekend. He and Megan had gone to Ikea to look at cribs. Not to buy them, just to look. Megan was still superstitious about buying too many things before the baby was born, even though every doctor's visit and ultrasound and screening had turned out okay. She'd been really tired, so they were in bed both Friday and Saturday by 9:00. He left this last part off and changed the subject. He really wanted to know about those keys. "What's with all the keys?"

"Clients," Stan said.

Clients? For an unemployed electrician? Maybe he'd changed fields, rebranded himself as a locksmith, a general contractor, a prison warden. "Business is booming?" Tate asked.

Stan picked up the wad of keys and jangled them, the rhino spinning and horning its way through the brass and silver and gold. "What's that sound like to you?" he asked.

"Keys?"

"Money," he said. "When times are tough, people fix up what they got. Decide they don't need that new house. Things are fine where they are with a fresh coat of paint or a new fixture. They hunker down and watch a lot of HGTV."

"If the nursery's not done yet," Dana said, "Stan can help."

Tate shook his head. "Megan doesn't want to jinx it," he said.

Stan tilted his milkshake glass at Tate. "Your life will never be the same."

Tate hated when people said shit like this, and a lot of people had been saying shit like this. *Get your rest! Go out now 'cause you'll never have a nice meal together again!* How did they know? Tate didn't get a good vibe from this guy, this strawberry milkshake-drinking, bald-domed, key jangler, and for some reason, he now felt protective of Dana, maybe because of her BFAW comment.

"Did you find what you were looking for, *Stanley*?" Tate elongated his name like it was an insult.

Stan took it like an insult and closed a suspect eye at Tate, a pop-eyed pirate. "It's Stan," he said. "Just Stan."

"Antiques," Tate said. "Did you find what you were looking for when you went ... 'antiquing.'" He used air quotes dramatically and judgmentally.

Dana put her arm around Stan. "He bought me a rocking chair," she said. "It's in pretty bad shape, but he can fix it." She leaned over and kissed him on his meatball-sized ear. "Stan's the man."

▼▼▼

After the playset there was more. Megan installed a ceiling fan in the bedroom because the summer was burning her up. She added a much-needed handrail down the stairs to the basement. She repaired the automatic garage door opener that had stopped being automatic and mounted the flat screen TV that had been propped precariously on top of their dresser. She cleaned out all the gutters. All this with apparent spectral assistance from Tate's father. She insisted he'd been talking to her, even going so far as to say that Tate's dad had gotten mad at her when she was mounting the TV.

"He was mean," she said.

"Mean?"

"Like if I did something wrong he got all frustrated."

Megan could not have known this about Tate's father. He'd always considered his dad pretty perfect, his hero really, but he had no patience when he was trying to help him or his brothers with a project. He was not a natural teacher. Whether it was how to add fractions or how to tie a hook on the end of a fishing line or how to fill a tire with air, if their dad was trying to teach them something and they couldn't understand, he'd get exasperated, huff and sigh, tell them he couldn't help them and give up, leaving them limply dangling a pencil, hook, or air pump.

Still, he stopped short of believing her.

"He could be like that," Tate said.

"I'm glad you're nothing like him," she said.

When she'd built a bookshelf—bought the wood, put it together, sanded and painted it herself—Tate finally understood the game. It didn't really matter how all the work was getting done. The point was for Tate to feel inadequate. Through the ghost of his dad she was showing Tate what he could be like, what he *should* be like, and what was missing from his dad-ness, all things he already knew and took too much to heart. This was an elaborately passive-aggressive way to point out Tate's flaws, but not unlike Megan.

So Tate fought back with pancakes. Not pancakes from the back of a box, but pancakes from scratch. The recipe was his mom's, one she'd come up with herself because she was a natural cook, a bona fide wizard in the kitchen, a mom who could bake anything, Super-mom, whip up a meal for five from a cupboard full of nothing.

Megan sat at the counter and listened to him as he easily and effortlessly moved around the kitchen, explaining where such a morning treat came from. For birthdays, good report cards, or even not-so-special occasions, his mom would make these pancakes, and when she poured them on the hot oiled skillet she would pour them in shapes, usually the first letter of their name, or maybe a long snake, or she'd try one in a spiral. His mom called them snake cakes. "And now I'm making them for you."

When the batter was mixed and ready, Tate oozed a long goopy strand on the electric skillet in the shape of the letter *M*. "You know what the *M* stands for?" he asked.

She didn't answer, her look implying it was obvious.

"Mom," he said.

Megan ate up the snake cakes without interpreting the gesture as an insult. She commented on how delicious they were, moist and buttery with hints of almond and orange zest, and how it would be great for him to make them one day for their kid, and how imagining that future scene made her want to cry from sweetness. Then she went ahead and cried.

So Tate made cupcakes. Again, nothing from a box, all from scratch. He found the recipe online. Some old lady in North Carolina calling herself Aunt Mabel and revealing all her family secrets on a blog. Tate told Megan that these cupcakes came from his own Great Aunt Mabel, a woman she'd never met, long dead, but a mother of seven who ran the family business—feed and seed—while still finding time to bake cupcakes and pies and cobblers and homemade bread, but especially these incredible cupcakes passed down from generation to generation, one mom to the next mom.

Megan bit into one, vanilla cake with a cream cheese frosting, rainbow sprinkles—his own touch. "Yum," she said.

She was clearly missing the point.

After the cupcakes, Tate made brownies. A fucking cornucopia of brownie varieties. He made them with pecans, butterscotch chips, chocolate chips, caramel swirls. He made blondies. He became a grand master of brownie, dusting them with powdered sugar and cutting them into perfect squares, crusty on the outside and moist on the inside. But Megan had lost her taste for chocolate during her pregnancy. She said it just didn't taste right. She nibbled at them politely, told him they were "nice." She said she liked his new baking hobby and she was well aware of what he was trying to prove. Fine. She couldn't bake. "Thanks for pointing out the obvious," she said.

"Who's going to bake his first birthday cake? His friends will want cookies. This is stuff a mom should know how to do."

"That's just like you."

"What?"

"A boy. You assume it'll be a boy."

Annabelle didn't look like either of them, lots of black hair and a big, flat nose. Nothing about her looked familiar. He remembered what his brother had said, when he'd asked Tate whether the baby was his, but all babies looked like aliens at first. She would change.

Megan's parents and Tate's mom both came to help out, staying in their small house for a week and a half, making it smaller. Tate was thankful to have them and even more thankful to finally see them go, even though Megan said she wasn't sure she'd know how to handle everything without them. Her mom told her she'd have to do it eventually, so the sooner the better. Surprisingly, Megan had decided to breastfeed.

She told him that a new father could sometimes feel left out observing the bond between the new mother and her nursing child. She'd read this. Much to his surprise, this was exactly how he did feel a lot of the time, useless and unimportant, watching Annabelle nurse then fall calmly to sleep in her mother's arms. Tate did as much as he could to help, but everything he did seemed to piss Annabelle off. She screamed when he tried to sponge bathe her, screamed when he bounced up and down the hall with her to stop her from screaming, and screamed when he read short books to her that she couldn't possibly understand or enjoy—Megan said it was important to start reading to her early. When his two weeks of leave were up, he was eager to get back to the office.

In his cube, he found an envelope resting on top of a small gift box. Inside the envelope was a card made out of pink construction paper, the front covered in glitter with cutout pictures of tiny winged pigs flying over a rustic farm scene. In paint pen across the top, bubble letters spelled out the word, "Congratulations!" Dana had made the card herself. He opened it up, and on the inside was a larger pig with wings, the same paint pen and bubble letters puffing out an inspirational phrase: "Believing is Seeing!" Tate flipped the card over to the back to see if there was more to it, but that was all.

It didn't make any sense. What was Dana trying to say? That Tate having a girl was like seeing a pig fly? That Tate being a dad was like a pig flying? And the saying, what the hell was that supposed to mean? All backwards. He didn't get it. He wanted to open the gift to see if it might help explain, but he decided to save it for Megan. He walked down to Dana's office to thank her and to ask her what she meant, but Zoe stopped him in the hallway.

"She's sick," Zoe said.

"Really?" Dana was never sick.

Zoe stuck a Cheetos-red finger between her teeth like she was thinking about something. "You have glitter on your face," she said.

At home, Megan unwrapped the gift from Dana and held up a small pink onesie with a flying pig on it. This didn't explain the card. There were no more words on the onesie, just a flying pig. Dana had also included one of her puppet key chains, a small, pink pig face. "Cute," Megan said, and added Dana's name to the long list of thank you notes she had to write.

After Dana was out sick for two more days, Zoe shared some gossip with the office. Stan was married and had two kids. He'd been living a double life. Dana was heartsick. Tate called Dana's phone and didn't get an answer. He left her a message saying he'd heard what had happened and was sorry, also thanking her for the card and the gift. Later in the day he called her again with no answer. On the third day Dana wasn't at work, Tate decided he'd go to her townhouse with brownies to thank her and to cheer her up. He was worried about her and figured she might need someone to talk to. He was her BFAW, after all.

Tate had only been to Dana's place once, that Halloween party last year. Megan lived for Halloween. They went as Frankenstein and the Bride of Frankenstein because they always did. He'd thought the party was going to be huge. Dana had made special invitations promising all kinds of fun and games and a big question mark announcing the wildness of an open-ended conclusion, but most of the people there weren't even in costume. The few who were looked like they'd just thrown their costumes together with a last minute stop at the drugstore: a plastic mask, nerd glasses, vampire teeth. Dana wore a sexy nurse's costume, and Tate thought she looked more desperate than sexy. It was obvious to him that she'd wanted to have a party to show herself off in that costume, to have all her friends see a side of her they might not have seen before. Tate wished someone else from the office had been there to see. Why was he the only one? Tate and Megan ended up talking to one of Dana's old law school friends who had given up law to travel around the world. He bragged about all the weird stuff he'd eaten: grubs, lizards, sheep's dick. Later the guy ended up vomiting in the bathroom and locking the door so no one could get in. One of Dana's other friends, some guy in an eye patch, found a mop bucket and pissed in it right in the kitchen, even though Dana had at least one other available bathroom. That's when Tate and Megan decided to leave. They'd been the youngest people there, but on the way home they talked about how it really hadn't seemed that way.

Outside Dana's place, Tate had to buzz three times before she answered and let him in. The townhouse smelled like someone had been sick in there, like that guy from the Halloween party was still hiding in her bathroom in a puddle of his own puke. Dana wore a pink track suit that made her look like a stick of chewing gum, already chewed. Her hair was flat and matted and her face was greasy, like she hadn't bathed all week. She was not glowing. Tate wondered if the rumors were just rumors and Dana really was sick, and here he was overstepping his boundaries as her legal assistant by coming to her house. He could leave her the brownies, thank her for the gift, and go.

Dana muted her TV and asked him to sit down on her couch, moving a rumpled afghan out of the way to give him room. She'd been watching an episode of *Three's Company*. Tate never understood how that show had ever been popular. TV was weird back then. Tate sat down and handed her the brownies wrapped in tinfoil. She told him he was sweet and that he shouldn't have brought her anything. He told her she shouldn't have made Annabelle anything, so they were even. Dana put the brownies down and snagged a Kleenex out of a box kept handy on her coffee table, a coffee table Tate remembered from the party. She'd decorated it herself, cut out pictures of old movie stars and lacquered over them on a cheap Salvation Army table. Marlon Brando was half-covered by wadded balls of dirty Kleenex.

"He says they're getting a divorce."

He'd been right about Stan. Never trust a guy with that many keys.

"You deserve better," Tate said.

Dana hugged him. She hugged him tightly in her yoga-strong arms, hugged him like somebody who hadn't seen a living soul in three days. "Too bad you don't have a brother," she said over his shoulder.

Tate wrapped his arms around Dana and slowly rubbed her back through her slick track suit. The thing to do was to go. He was in another woman's home, an emotional woman, a vulnerable woman, a woman not wearing a bra. He concentrated on the TV, where Don Knotts was giving a fish face to John Ritter.

Both of those guys were dead now.

When Tate kissed Dana on the neck, she shivered, but she didn't stop him, so he kissed her neck again, and Dana tilted her head to the side to give him a wider target, so he moved from her neck to her ear back to her neck to her lips, where her tongue rushed inside his mouth like a burst of warm water, and he leaned her back into the couch, clutching her wrist, pressing her hard into the cushions, on top of the afghan, her legs scissoring around him and their hips aligning bone on bone, and they humped like teenagers, her thin track suit easing the friction, until she freed her wrist and plunged her hand down the front of Tate's pants, her palm stroking him quickly, until he came quickly, and she turned her face away from his so that he accidentally licked her. She tasted like a pretzel.

"Ouch," Dana said. "Something's poking me in the..." She reached under her back with her free hand and pulled out one of her dolls, apparently unfinished, needles sticking everywhere, thread dangling off like wisps of hair. She laughed and held it up to him. "Steve McQueen."

Tate felt ridiculous.

Dana eased her hand out of his pants, cupping it like she held something precious.

Tate sat up.

Dana yanked out three, four Kleenexes and wiped off her hand.

"I have two older brothers," he said.

Dana stood up. "Be right back," she said, the wad of Kleenex clutched in her fist. "Don't go. Please."

Tate picked up the doll. He didn't know what Dana was doing, where she was going, whether she was washing her hands, taking a shower, changing into her sexy nurse's costume, calling Zoe at work to spread the gossip of what had just gone down, but he didn't wait to find out. The doll freaked him out. It looked more like himself than Steve McQueen, more like a Tate voodoo doll. He took it and ran.

Before he went home, Tate stopped at a bar. He went into the bathroom and scrubbed his hands with soap and water, his face too, over his neck, splashing the water all over his shirt, into his hair, a clipped bird thrashing in a bath. Work was going to suck. He gulped down a beer and a shot and then asked for a pint glass full of ice water. He drank it and immediately asked for another, as if enough water could dissolve what he'd just done. He left the puppet upside down in the glass, head first, like the tinier Tate had guzzled all the water himself.

He felt better after the bar, buzzed and light, dreamy, a feeling that only grew when he got home and couldn't find the girls anywhere. He called both their names and searched all over the house. Megan's slippers stood a stride apart in the hallway. The washing machine churned in the basement. In the kitchen, a glass sat half-filled with milk next to a plate littered with the crumbs of a brownie. Her taste for chocolate had come back. The stroller was propped in the foyer, and the baby carrier was empty, a blanket piled in it along with a pacifier as if the baby had vaporized. Megan's car was in the garage. The way everything looked, still and abandoned, interrupted, made it seem like they'd suddenly and mysteriously vanished, as if they'd gotten sucked up in the middle of whatever they were doing.

Maybe Megan hadn't been making all that up about his dad, and he could do more than teach her how to be handy. He could tell on his son, come to Megan and say, in his ghostly Johnny Cash drawl, "Hey, Tate's foolin' around on you." And maybe when Tate looked in his backyard he was going to see proof, proof of all the supernatural shit his wife had been believing, his dad behind the wheel of the ship he'd helped build, getting ready to steer his family toward the clouds, to spirit them away some place far from Tate, and he could run out in the yard and tell him to wait, wave his arms and yell up to the ship, *wait!*, ask his dad all the questions he'd never gotten answers to.

Leaving Charity

Clark came over to my house dressed like he was headed to a fiesta, flowery shirt, shorts below his knees, flip flops. He had his video camera with him and set it on top of a tripod before sliding one of my deck chairs between the camera and the pool.

"Stand in for me," he said.

I sat down in the chair, figuring that's what he meant. He fine-tuned and wiggled the camera parts, doing whatever it is that people do who are skilled at looking at things through cameras. Clark was a real cinematographer. At least *I* thought so. He would never claim that title for himself because he said nothing he'd filmed had ever made it to the cinema. But everything I'd seen was good, and what he'd done for my store was like the *Star Wars* of furniture advertising. Sure, he could border on annoying when he got to harping on the way light looked and how different colors created mood and shadows played artsy-fartsy, blah, blah, blah. But shooting stuff was the one area where Clark seemed to know what the hell he was doing. Like now, he kept asking me to shift positions, scooch left, angle the chair, lift my head up, all until I was like he wanted me, facing directly into the sun and squinting so tightly I could barely see.

"Take a look," he said.

I switched places with him and stuck my eyeball to the camera. Inside I saw a tiny image of Clark sitting in the chair cross-legged. His mirrored sunglasses reflected bright sunbursts in its lenses. My pool was gleaming behind him, the fruitless banana tree Carol planted behind that. When she bought it, I asked her what the point of a banana tree was if it didn't make bananas. *Ambience*, she said, in a Frenchy way. Even though I was still irritated she stuck that thing out there in the middle of the nice flower beds I'd already made, the shot did have something to it. Clark looked like a star taking a pool break in Malibu or some such place.

"What do you think?"

I took my eye off the camera and shrugged.

"Yep. Needs a little something," he said. Then he slapped his palms on his thighs and went inside my house.

I looked back at the image of the empty chair, the banana tree, the water of my pool looking cool and still, waiting for somebody to jump in. When we were young, we used to hurl Nerf footballs above the Eechacohee public pool, each one of us attempting miraculous mid-air catches before splashing down into the water. Clark could catch them behind his back, under his legs, upside down. He could pull off a flip and snatch the water-logged Nerf ball right out of its heavy fall. But a lot of times he'd end up kneeing or elbowing an unsuspecting head on his way down, sending three-year-olds flapping their floaty arms and crying to their mamas. A dream of mine then was to own my own pool someday, closed to the public, the only swimmers being my family and those I invited. My oasis. Of course, Clark considered himself invited all the time; then again, he was almost family. I didn't know what he was up to now, but it seemed like my pool was necessary.

Clark came back out carrying two tall glasses with cocktail umbrellas. He handed me one, then dragged my small glass top table next to the deck chair, placing his drink on top before sitting down. I took a sip. It tasted sweet and kind of alcoholic. I asked him what it was.

"Mai tai," he said. "Adds to the *mise-en-scene*."

I took that to be the same as ambience. It surprised me that there was stuff inside the house to make mai tais, including colorful little cocktail umbrellas. I thought Carol had gotten rid of all the liquor once she got pregnant again. She said she didn't have enough willpower to keep it around the house. I didn't understand why both of us had to suffer.

"Okay. Push the red button and say 'speed'."

I looked in the camera again to make sure nothing had moved. The mai tai on the table hadn't changed things as far as I could see. I pushed the record button and said "speed," for whatever reason, and after I did, he took a dramatic gulp of his mai tai and crossed one leg over the other before starting in.

"Hello Mac — shit. Cut." Clark waved his hands in the air. "Sorry. Take two."

I'm Mac. Short for MacArthur. My daddy admired the General, or at least Gregory Peck's version of him.

"Okay." Clark re-situated himself in the chair and shook his head like a wet dog. "When it's rolling, say 'speed'."

He took another big gulp of his mai tai before take two.

"Speed."

"Hello, Louise." Louise was his mama, but I'd never known him to call her by her first name. She'd probably slap him. "I'm leaving," he said into the camera. "I'm in love with Mary Beth, and we're moving to California."

I laughed. Clark had been trying to leave his mama's house, the tired town that was Charity, the state of Georgia, the South, for all of his thirty-one years. But he didn't have it in him. In the end, the free roof over his head, the home cooking, and the undying support of friends like me were always too much to give up. I was positive this latest effort would end the same way.

"You remember, Mama? When Mac and I were ... say 'Hey,' Mac."

I stuck my fingers in front of the camera and said, "Hey."

Clark continued, "Remember? That sweltering summer before our senior year when Mac and I decided to skip football camp because we couldn't take the heat? From past experience we knew how the heat at camp would envelop you like an extra layer of suffocating clothes, and the gnats, dear God the gnats, phalanxes of gnats would big-bang into black planets that orbited the seething sun of your helmet, and the spy-quick mosquito stings and grass blade slices made you want to claw your skin off."

Clark had obviously written and memorized this script. I didn't know why he was telling this story. His mama knew how it ended. Or why he couldn't just say it was hot and get on with it. Or why he couldn't tell her he was leaving in person and light out.

He kept on with the story. "By our youthful estimation, we figured if we skipped camp, disappeared, only to return immediately before school, the punishment would be swift and keen, but as the football team would be lacking without our considerable talents, they would have to let us suit up. So, we absconded with your LeSabre, and westward we drove to virgin vistas, parting the flat country, as flat as far is far, the stripped land punctuated only by a silver silo or a bleak barn erupting out of the earth like bruised fingers and thumbs."

We drove west.

"Then, after a couple of days of freedom, the mountains stopped us. And in my melancholy memory, those mountains still rise up like a postcard image, somehow unreal through the windshield, like a half-mad artist had painted a big sheet in front of us with perfect details of the fake landscape. I remember thinking, Mama, that if we drove through it, kept going, we might fall off the edge into a deep abyss. We didn't touch the mountains. We didn't *climb* the mountains. We couldn't press forward. We couldn't—"

Blah, blah, blah. We got caught. We were sleeping in the car in a state park in Wheeler, Arizona. We weren't supposed to sleep in this park, which probably wouldn't have been that big of a deal to Officer Rispin, who found us there, had I not started running my mouth and confessing to everything. I told him we'd stolen Clark's mama's car, that we were running away from football camp, and even that an old man had bought us beer back in Gallup. I don't know why I said all that. I guess I was tired of driving.

The Wheeler police station had one of those holding cells you see on TV shows for Otis-type town drunks, but Officer Rispin either wouldn't or couldn't keep us in there, so we stayed in the breakroom. He put sleeping bags down and fed us Cup-a-Soups and frozen bagels. Clark would forever claim he was a hardened ex-con because of this experience. His mama flew to Phoenix. Officer Rispin escorted us all the way down there in the LeSabre. She thanked him, threw us in, and drove back east, wearing our ears out about responsibility and making us listen to Norman Vincent Peale tapes on the cassette player. The trip ended our football careers. Clark never blamed me.

Instead, I guess he blamed the mountains, like he was doing now. He kept talking and waving his hands in front of the camera for a good five more minutes about those mountains and how they had provided him with what he called "an epiphany." He said it was the moment he discovered there were parts of this thing called life that were not total bullshit, and he believed

California still held the promise of what was beyond those mountains, and Mary Beth, beautiful jailbait Mary Beth—he left that out—had convinced him it was about time he get on with it, that they fulfill their California dreams together, because only by diving in to the free flowing Pacific ocean of their dreams could they see what the water was like.

I pushed the record button to stop his nonsense.

I wanted to remind him that our trip was a long time ago. When we didn't have much sense and even less responsibility. And that about the only responsibility we did have was owed to our teammates, and we couldn't even live up to that—just like his mama had said. And that Mary Beth was too young to think straight and would probably dump him the minute she met Kevin Costner. And that California was a long way away. And that a videotape was not the right way to say goodbye to anybody.

But before I could say anything, he pulled his sunglasses down on the bridge of his nose and said, "Turn the camera back on, Mac." His eyes were bloodshot, like he'd been crying behind his glasses or smoking pot before he came over—either one was a possibility.

"What for?" I asked.

Clark stood up from the deck chair and came to me slowly. He put his hand on my shoulder. "I need your help." Then his eyes started to well up, and I knew I would do whatever he wanted.

What he said he wanted was for me to finish taping this scene by the pool and then follow him to his house where he was going to videotape all his belongings. For evidence, he said.

"Evidence of what?"

"Possession," he said. "So the movers don't fuck it up."

I told him that was really smart, but truthfully I couldn't see any of this quite working out the way he planned.

He sat back down and finished up his speech, and then we walked down the street to his house. His mama had gone out to eat fish with Mr. Ken, but Clark said she might be back soon, so we had to hurry. He switched the tapes out and started zooming around the living room, the kitchen, his bedroom, while I followed him with the camera.

"This is my couch." It was actually his mama's couch, but I guess he figured since it had been the site over the years for so much of his horniness and leisure, he'd earned it. He stood still, his legs straight, but with his upper body kind of tilted to the side like a broken street sign. An outstretched finger pointed at the couch. He held the pose long enough for me to ask what he was doing.

"I want to make sure there's no confusion."

I asked him why he didn't just stick notes on everything.

Clark looked at me like I was being stupid. "Because she'll take them off."

He kept this act up around the rest of the house, pointing at his stuff, doing different poses each time. Sometimes he would bend on one knee, sometimes he would point with both hands, sometimes he would lift something light above his head saying, "This. This magnificent vase is mine." It was an odd spectacle and one that did not seem wholly sane.

When he was done, he took the tape out and wrote on a thin white label for the spine: MOVERS. He ran the label along the side of the tape, making sure it stuck; then he did the same thing with the first tape, writing MOM on a thin strip and labeling it too.

"You're really making a production here," I said.

"Yep," he said. Then he went into his bedroom and shut the door.

I sat down on the couch. It had seen better days, but I didn't want to think about any of them. I started thinking instead about Carol and what she'd say about all this. She'd known Clark as long as I had. I wanted to call her and tell her, see if she could give me something smart to say, but she'd probably be all for it. She'd probably say the two of us could use the separation and that Clark was a man-child who needed to grow up. Sometimes she acted like she didn't like Clark, but that wasn't true.

I thought about last summer when she lost our first baby and how upset she was. I was too, but it happened to lots of women, so I didn't think it was the end of the world. Now Carol was pregnant again and everything was fine. But after the first one she stayed in our bedroom with the door shut, watching game shows all day. You would think that a nurse would be able to handle such natural tragedies. It wasn't like she wouldn't let me in. The door wasn't locked, but she was unresponsive, just staring at old "Match Games" and "$25,000 Pyramids." After several days of this, Clark came over to visit. I was out by the pool, situating the new automatic vacuum I'd bought. He went inside for no more than five minutes before he came back out, took his shirt off, and laid out in one of my lounge chairs for the rest of the afternoon.

That night, Carol came out of the bedroom. We ordered Chinese food and talked. I couldn't figure it out. Something had happened to change her attitude.

"What'd he say?" I asked.

"Who?"

"Clark."

"Nothing really."

"Well he had to have said *something*."

I raised my voice despite myself. I had been no help. I thought I'd catered to her every need, brought her home decorating magazines and Ibuprofen, the lime flavored fizzy water she liked. I'd offered to rub her feet, to rub her back, to do whatever she wanted that would snap her out of the funk, but I couldn't do it. But you know what Clark brought her? Straws. Multi-colored bendable straws. He told her he remembered when we were kids and Carol was really sick, laying out of school for over a week, and he was the one who had to bring all her homework to her. He told her he always remembered her in her daddy's chair, a blanket pulled up to her chin, and her lips permanently attached to one of those bendy straws stuck into the hole of a Coca-Cola can. For some reason this straw story struck a chord.

Carol could tell I was kind of put out to realize that Clark could walk into our bedroom with straws and suddenly lift her up. She told me not to worry about it. That I'd been perfect throughout the whole ordeal and that, besides the straws, Clark didn't really say anything different than I'd already said. "He just has a way of putting it," she said.

Clark came back out of his bedroom wearing a seersucker suit and carrying a large leather duffel bag, grinning.

"How do I look?"

I felt like I'd said enough, so I told him he looked great and we moved on.

The next thing we were doing was for me, he said. I was going to carry him to see Mary Beth at the Walgreens, where she was presently quitting her job. He wanted me to shoot the whole thing on video so I had it to remember the moment, him looking his happiest, on the road to California. Together, he and Mary Beth would climb in her Jeep and ride off into the sunset, headed west. "Like Thelma and Louise," he said.

I reminded him that Thelma and Louise drove off a cliff.

"Holding hands," he said.

We walked back to my place, grabbed the car, and drove to Walgreens. He told me not to use the tripod this time but to just hold the camera because that was more like real life. Mary Beth strutted outside with a checkered scarf tied on the top of her head and giant sunglasses shielding her eyes from the dimming sun, dressed like she was the next big Hollywood thing. I guess she thought she was. They kissed, and she kicked a bare calf up underneath her knee-length skirt.

"Hey, sport," she said to me.

Real life, my ass. I shut off the camera.

"Are you for real?"

Clark nodded and so did Mary Beth, even though I wasn't talking to her.

"Have you thought about the consequences here?" The minute I said it I knew I sounded stupid and that he would definitely mention that while also denying the fact he cared about any consequences.

But he didn't say anything. He hugged me, and as dumb as all this was, as much as I thought he'd turn around and be back within a day or two, I got a fist in my throat that made me feel like an idiot.

He took the camera from me and popped out the tape and wrote out another label on a thin white strip. LEAVING CHARITY. He started writing it too big, so he had to squeeze all the last letters together in a mess at the far end of the label. Then he put the tape back in the camera and handed it to me.

He needed me to do one more thing, he said. The camera was for me, a parting gift for helping him out so much and for sticking by him, being a true friend. I was to use the camera to shoot my baby growing up, walking and talking and going to kindergarten, so Carol and I would have its whole childhood on tape for posterity. But also, and this was the big one, his mama and the movers needed a way to watch those tapes with their names on them, and the only way they could do that was with the camera. So, if I could be a good friend, and, recognizing the true generosity of the gift, show them the tapes using the camera that was now mine, that'd be great. He flipped out a small panel on the side of the camera and said I could either hook the whole camera up to the TV, or I could let them watch through the small side panel. Thanks.

He gave me another hug and threw his bag in the back of Mary Beth's Jeep before climbing in the passenger's side.

The little tart kissed me on the cheek. "He's going to miss you," she whispered.

Then Mary Beth got behind the wheel, and I pushed the button to shoot them again. I thought at least there might be something instructive in all this for my unborn kid, a lesson about selfishness and foolishness and spectacle to show the kid at a later date as warning and instruction. Hey, don't grow up to be an asshole like your Uncle Clark, sticking your best friend with responsibilities you don't have the balls to handle while you run off to chase your washed-up dreams with a fresh piece of ass.

I yelled "speed" and looked into the camera.

It was spectacular. It was spectacular because at that moment, watching them drive away, what I saw was exactly out of a movie. The sky was half-dark, a deep blue curtain closing down the day, ending the show, and faded and far away, the heart of the moon just started beating through the velvety cloak of coming dark, and all the street colors were flashing and popping below, the camera-eyes of red taillights, the electric yellows and blazing greens of the stretch of consumer strip, Charity, Exit 137, an endless line of fast food chains and gas stations and Coca-Cola pit stops and bright flying car alloys, and above it all, between the curtain and the cars was this brilliant sunset, a gorgeous sunset with no rhyme or reason to it, like long, twisted lengths of film, ribboning out in curls of color— orange, purple, and lipstick pink—stretching and unfurling, pressing to stay lit up, on screen, illuminated forever against the darkening of the blah, blah, blah.

Everything is Going to be Okay

Maria is worried about the future, which has Doug worried because usually his wife is never worried. He blames it on the pregnancy, then hates himself for being that kind of guy. Recently she has been calling him, sending him text messages, posting on his Facebook wall, emailing him with dismal news about the gloomy world their child will face. By the year 2030, college tuition will reach the staggering price of $$$$$ per year. Why didn't they start saving earlier? The *Chicago Tribune* reports that gang-related violence in Humboldt Park has risen five percent in the past six months. Should they think about moving? A twelve-year-old in Texas shot his parents while they were asleep because he'd been grounded from his PlayStation right before a very important Halo tournament. Isn't that the game Doug plays after she falls asleep? They should get rid of it.

Today she leaves him a voicemail message with the news their brains are dying. Researchers have found that constantly interfacing with personal technology is literally killing our brains, and with each new leap forward our humanity is sliding back. We no longer charge that part of the brain that teaches us to talk to one another, socialize, carry on a conversation that doesn't involve emoticons, acronyms, and egregious misspellings. As a result, we are breeding a race of over-stimulated, short-attention-spanned, solitary, techno-zombies who, she says, "can hold blockbuster movies in the palm of their hand but don't know how to hold each other." Doug cannot believe this is Maria, a woman with two degrees, founder and director of a successful non-profit (PBJ, a pit bull rehabilitation center and no-kill shelter), a smart and talented woman, who sends him such warnings using these same "brain-murdering" methods without any sense of irony. He texts her back, making sure to spell out all the words, "Everything is going to be okay."

Doug is in the middle of an editing session, a hyper-stylized thirty second promo for an upcoming special on steroids in professional sports—a subject Maria would probably also find portentous—when his cell phone rings. Normally Doug doesn't answer his phone during an editing session, but his wife is pregnant and recently over-worried, so he's made it okay. He looks behind him at the producer sitting on the leather couch. He is asleep. Doug likes to edit when his producers fall asleep. They stay out of the way and let him do his job. When he picks up his cell phone, he is surprised to see that the screen does not say "Maria" but "Julie." He can't remember the last time he talked to his sister. She doesn't make a habit of calling and never calls during the day. Something must be wrong.

He answers. "What's wrong?"

"Where do you live?" she asks. She is talking on speaker phone in her car, the wind rushing an ambient whoosh through the open windows, making it so she has to yell.

"Chicago," he says.

"No shit. What's the address?"

Doug can hear country music whining in the background. He and Julie have never had the same taste in music. He tells her his address, then hears her navigation system advise her to stay straight. Julie lives 700 miles away in the suburbs of Atlanta. "What are you doing?" he asks.

"Sending you a letter," she says, then the sound of the wind and the car and the country music are gone.

The conversation is weird, but so is his sister.

Doug hits the space bar and plays the promo he's been working on from the beginning. After thirty seconds of quick cuts, bumping electronic music, and synched-up sound effects on every crack of bat, crunch of pads, and swish of net, the producer wakes up and tells Doug he doesn't like the music anymore.

"What's wrong with it?" Doug asks.

"I don't know," the producer says. "It's too ..." he slaps the back of his hand into his palm, three quick slaps, "... something."

Later in the afternoon, Doug gets another call. The phone screen says "Dad," but when he answers it's Maxine, his dad's second wife. "Sister's missing," she says.

Maxine names everyone according to their roles in the family, like they're characters in a Tennessee Williams play. Doug hates this. "Missing what?"

"That's not funny," Maxine says, and Doug can picture the look on her face, eyes saucer wide, lips puckered like a lipsticked anus. "She didn't pick the kids up from school. Corey's been calling her. She won't answer."

None of these facts mean Julie is missing. He wonders what Maxine expects him to do about it. "I don't know what to tell you," he says. It occurs to him that he might need to cover for Julie—maybe she's done something she needs to hide from, robbed a liquor store, shot a would-be-rapist in the face, left a trail of crimes followed by a column of troopers. You could never tell with Julie.

"You're her brother," Maxine says.

Again, Doug doesn't know the intentions behind such an obvious statement. "If I hear from her, I'll let you know," he says.

Maxine squawks out "You—" before Doug's thumb ends the conversation.

By the time he and Maria go to bed, he has not heard from Julie again. A neighbor's porch light makes their bedroom brighter than either he or Maria like, perpetual dusk. He's told

Maria he's close enough to shoot it out with a BB gun. She says it would probably be more neighborly to go talk to them. In the not-quite dark, Doug stares at the rotating ceiling fan, turns on his right side, tries to keep his eyes closed to not look at the clock, turns to his left side, stares at his sleeping wife, Maria, peaceful and beautiful, thinks how cliché he is for staring at his sleeping wife, Maria, peaceful and beautiful, flips on his back and re-stares at the rotating ceiling fan. He is surprised to be so worried. He feels like his dad. Julie has kept their dad awake a billion nights with worry. Doug senses that this will be the rest of his life after their baby is born, a dad, forever awake in the half dark, no sleep, never again, psychotic with worry. He tries to convince himself that Julie was joking, that she punched in his address on her navigation system just to see how far Chicago was, that she really did intend to send him a letter or a package or a cookie bouquet just because she was thinking of him, that she's back at home, asleep next to Corey, who is rolling over and staring at her in the dark, peaceful and beautiful, just as much of a cliché as Doug. But Doug is not convinced.

At two in the morning, the condo buzzer goes off. From his dog bed, Brick barks until Doug tells him to hush. Brick is built just like a brick, squat and rectangular, solid, rust-colored. A Wendy's employee found him starving by the dumpster, maggot-covered wounds on his chest. Maria saved him, brought him home. Doug does not immediately move for the door. Sometimes there are prank buzzers in the middle of the night, neighborhood kids flattening their hands across buttons on their high walks home. The buzzer buzzes again. Brick looks at Doug, waiting for approval to run to the door and bark himself hoarse. In a sleepy voice, Maria tells Doug to go see who it is. Earlier that night, over Thai takeout, Doug had told Maria about his weird conversation with his sister, but Maria knows Julie too and agreed that it was probably just her bad idea of a joke. In his boxers, with Brick following, Doug hurries from the bedroom to the front door, to the intercom on the wall, hits the talk button, says hello.

"It's scary as fuck out here," Julie's voice crackles through the intercom. Doug feels like he's in a dream. "Let me in."

Doug buzzes her in, opens the front door, and walks into the stairwell. Looking over the rail, he can see her brown and blond highlighted hair bouncing hurriedly up the stairs. As far as he can tell she's not carrying a suitcase, just what looks like a deep pocketed purse slung over her shoulder, so Doug doesn't go down to help. He figures she would yell for help if she needed it. "Third floor," he says.

"You would," she says.

When she reaches the top, she's out of breath, and Doug thinks she looks tired. She has no makeup on. Julie always wears makeup. She's doesn't go grocery shopping without makeup. Her khaki shorts are what he considers too short for his sister, for a mom, a forty-year-old woman, and her black V-neck shirt plunges too low, revealing the wide and ample freckled space between her wide and ample fake boobs. When she hugs him, Doug angles to the side to avoid meeting her chest to chest. Ever since she got those boobs Doug has been uncomfortable hugging her. That was ten years ago. Doug was twenty-two. He remembers thinking at the time that Julie was not going to let herself get old, and that new boobs were the first of many measures meant to counter her inevitable aging. He's not sure what all she's had done since then, but tonight her teeth look as bright as his neighbor's porch light.

Inside the condo, Brick clips across the hardwood and nudges his muscled head under Julie's hand. They have never met. Doug thinks people are wrong to be so afraid of pit bulls. "Nice neighborhood," she says, petting Brick's head. "Can I leave my car parked on the street or is it gonna get jacked?"

Maria is standing in the living room, sleepy-eyed, with a threadbare 1995 Big Pig Jig Barbecue T-shirt draped over her growing body. Maria is a vegetarian. "It's not that bad," she says. She's sensitive about the neighborhood and likes it the way it is. When she and Doug first moved, she did not want them to appear like yuppies gentrifying Humboldt Park. She signed them up for Spanish lessons and started shopping at the Carniceria y Fruteria. Maria's dad is Puerto Rican, but, wanting to fully integrate, did not speak Spanish at home. For similar reasons, he pushed her into tennis. Now his daughter is trying to reverse the process.

She tells Julie there's a towel for her in the front bathroom and asks her if she needs anything else. Julie says no thanks, and Maria slides sweetly on bare feet back to the bedroom, Brick following, where she shuts the door behind them both. Doug loves this about Maria. She stays out of other people's business until she's asked or forced to jump in. Her family is just the opposite.

Julie slings her purse on the floor and collapses, face first, onto the sofa.

"Want a drink?" Doug asks.

Julie doesn't answer. Sitting next to her on the sofa, he puts his hand on her shoulder. She is too thin. She is not shuddering or shaking, but Doug can tell she's crying. He can smell it. Since he was five, Doug has believed he has the power to smell Julie's moods. Grapes mean she's happy. Spaghetti means she's scared. Dirty laundry means she's upset. He has never told anyone this, not even Maria, and sometimes he doesn't believe it himself. But even with the windows cracked, and the cool Midwestern May carrying in city scents—fried foods, dog poop, blooms and sewers—Doug's certain he can smell sweaty socks.

▼▼▼

On Saturday mornings Doug and Maria like to get up and stake claim to a tennis court in Humboldt Park. When they wake up, Maria asks him if they're keeping their date. Maria is a fanatic about tennis. Whacking a ball around the court calms her, loosens a week's worth of tension. Tennis is her therapy, she says, but much cheaper. She tries to play three times a week, but Saturdays with Doug are the most important, the date she won't let slide. Even though Doug knows not playing might ruin Maria's weekend, he hopes that his sister will want to talk this morning, let her brother in on the secret of her visit, confide in him. Last night Julie had only told him she was tired and wanted to sleep, so he didn't press the issue. He'd showed her to their guest bedroom, the soon-to-be baby's room, where, luckily, the futon was still there ready for her. Doug and Maria have had arguments about keeping the futon, but he's lost them all.

"Let's play it by ear," he says. Maria nudges him out of the bed with her still slender feet. He wonders when and if they'll get fat.

When Doug walks into the kitchen, he's surprised to see Julie already awake, sitting at a barstool, his laptop open in front of her on the countertop. The kitchen smells of coffee. Julie has helped herself. He's glad she feels at home. Through the tiny speakers on the computer, Doug hears a tiny voice. "Daddy's mad," the voice says. It's Doug's niece Charlotte. Doug does not like her name or her brother's—Harvey. They are both too old-fashioned. He has told Maria that they aren't going to choose an old-fashioned name for their child, that he wants something new, something forward-looking, original and futuristic, like Brace or Steen. They are having a child, not writing a sci-fi novel, Maria informs him. Doug wonders why Julie's using Skype instead of her phone.

"He's just grumpy," Julie says.

"You didn't tell him," Charlotte says.

"Ask him if he's my daddy."

"He's outside."

"Want to say 'hey' to your uncle?"

Doug grabs the coffee carafe and a mug before looking over Julie's shoulder. He pours himself a cup. On the computer screen, captured in a small square, a wide mouth with its front teeth missing opens and closes over the camera eye, moaning, "Haaaaa-looooow, haaaaa-looooow, haaaa-looooow."

"Hey, Charlotte," Doug says.

The mouth closes and moves back from the camera. A purple ring circles her lips, sticky, like she's been guzzling Kool-Aid. She already looks older than the last time Doug saw her at Christmas. Everybody seemed okay then. Kids are honest. They shoot straight, tell you you've got spinach in your teeth when your friends won't. Doug asks Charlotte, "What's your mama doing in Chicago?"

"She needed a break," Charlotte says.

"We gotta go," Julie says. "Tell your brother I love him."

Charlotte turns her head and yells, "Har-vey! Mama loves you!" then turns her head back, facing the camera. "Where's Maria?"

"On a rocket ship to Pluto," Doug says.

"Pluto's not even a planet."

"So? You can still go there, Miss Smarty Britches."

"Uh-uh."

"Yeah-huh."

"Uh-uh."

While they argue, Maria comes out of the bedroom dressed for tennis, neon yellow visor, black skirt, long-sleeved black shirt with a neon yellow pattern that swirls on her small round belly like a hurricane. So much for playing it by ear. Behind Doug's shoulder, she stands on her tennis-shoed tiptoes and waves to Charlotte in the computer. "Good morning, Charlotte," she says, then takes the coffee carafe from Doug and places it back on the burner.

"Ha!" Charlotte shouts. "Told you!"

"She hasn't left yet," Doug says. "Aren't you going to Pluto later?"

Maria is pouring herself a glass of orange juice and doesn't answer.

"We're all going to Pluto," Julie says. "Right now. Bye, baby. Love you."

Charlotte waves her hand in front of the camera like she's trying to shake a booger off her fingers. She blows purple Kool-Aid kisses left and right. "Love you. Love you. Love you," she says, a jewel off the drama queen's crown. Her face shoots close to the camera eye again. "Send me a postcard from Pluto, Mama."

"Yes ma'am." Julie closes the laptop and checks out Maria sipping from her juice glass.

Maria catches Julie staring at her. "What?" she asks.

"Black is slimming on you," Julie says.

▼▼▼

Before they can go, Doug has to walk Brick around the block, which Julie takes to mean she's got time to get ready. She showers for what feels like a good half hour, blow dries her hair to hay, painstakingly puts on makeup, and takes her time debating which color nylon sports jacket—aqua or chocolate brown—to borrow from Maria and wear over the same V-neck and shorts combo she had on last night. Doug wonders if Julie has brought any more clothes in her purse, or if she just dropped the kids off at school, told them she was going to Chicago for the weekend, and kept on driving, on a whim, fed up. The conversation with Charlotte has made Doug less worried. At least her family knows where she is, but he'd still like to know why where she is is with him.

The morning is nice for May, not too cool, already warming. Maria walks a few strides ahead, most likely convinced the extra time Julie has taken will mean all the courts are full. Doug hauls the tennis bag on his shoulder while Julie walks empty-handed, her purse strap carving a diagonal strip through the swells in her lake-colored jacket. Her flip-flops flap as she hums a song that sounds familiar, one that Doug can't quite make out.

"Are you humming Jimmy Buffett?" Maria asks, her chin cocked sharply over her shoulder, looking back.

"I can't get it out of my head," Julie says. "They say you've got to sing a whole song through to get rid of it, but nobody ever knows the whole song. That's why it gets stuck." She sings, "*Wastin' away again in Margaritaville*—"

Maria interrupts. "I hate Jimmy Buffett."

Doug can't help but think Julie is dropping clues, hinting at something in the song that provides reasons for why she's here. For the first time in his life, Doug wishes he knew all the lyrics to "Margaritaville."

Luckily, one court is open when they arrive. As the due date speeds closer—September 13th—and Maria gets more uncomfortable, Doug fears the inevitable end of tennis. He doesn't know what to expect from her then, how her attitude will change, but worse than that, and he hates himself for even thinking it, he fears what will happen to her physically. He knows. He's a terrible person, but the thought more than crosses his mind, it takes up residence and squats. He tells himself it won't matter, that they could be a fat and happy family together and that would be great. But Maria is Maria because of her body. Doug has never known anyone else like her, an athlete, a *real* athlete, an athlete-athlete, a person so intimately connected in mind and body. Doug tries to flip his ugly fears positively, rationalize them not in terms of physical attraction, but in terms of mental activity and grace. He does not fear Maria getting less hot; he fears her getting dull. But no matter how he spins it, he still hates himself for thinking like a pig.

Maria pulls a can of fresh balls out of their tennis bag and peels it open. She keeps two balls in her hand and wedges another into the elastic under her skirt, a move Doug has always and still does find incredibly sexy. "I can't play very long," Maria tells Julie.

Julie is sitting on a bench facing the morning sun, huge sunglasses covering her face like solar panels. She unzips her borrowed jacket. "Take your time," she says. The scene is surreal to Doug, his sister sitting on a bench in Humboldt Park. Until she punched his address into her navigation system, he's positive she didn't know exactly where Chicago was.

When Doug and Maria first started playing tennis together, they kept score, but he could never beat her, so trying to became less fun. Now they simply volley with no points or games on the line, Doug hitting the ball where Maria wants it so she can practice her forehands, backhands, net play, serves. A glorified ball machine. On the court, the time from Doug's thought to physical action seems like minutes, muddy slow motion, but Maria is always on her toes, running to the right place before he even hits the ball, like her body can see the future. But today Doug can see she's slowing down.

After only fifteen minutes of volleying, Maria is ready to practice her serves. Typically, this is Doug's least favorite part. When she's on, her serves are lethal, and most of the time he simply stands there and lets the ball fly by, or, when he is able to get his racquet on it, ends up misfiring over the fence or squirting the ball onto the adjacent court. He doesn't really even need to be there, only she says she wants someone to aim at. Julie can stand there as easily as he can. Doug asks her if she wants to play. She has her legs out, long and crossed at the ankle, her arms stretched wide over the back of the bench catching the sun. Julie raises her right leg up and, flexing her toes, slaps her flip-flop against her heel. "I'll have a blow out," she says.

Doug bounces on his toes in the deuce court, ready to receive. Maria's first serve hits the net. It's difficult watching her try to put her whole body into it. A motion that once was so fluid for her has turned awkward. She tosses and serves again, this time over the net, and he returns it easily. Her serve has no juice to it. Still, Maria seems surprised that he's gotten it back to her, a well-paced return. She doesn't have to move much and rockets a forehand down the line, obviously angry at her weak serve, but Doug sees it coming and is in position to hit a soft backhand.

Julie starts singing, loudly, *"Lookin' for my lost shaker of salt.* He's really a good song writer," she says.

Doug wants to laugh, but the volley has suddenly turned serious. Julie must recognize it too and is trying to help him by distracting Maria with a song she hates. It only makes Maria more competitive. She tries to go cross court on him, but he runs the ball down. He does not know why he's continuing to play this point, to reach for every ball, but he hits a perfect drop shot that Maria is not expecting. She is out of position and galumphs to the net in chase. It is difficult to watch, graceful Maria galumphing. He worries for a minute she's going to fall, and Doug pictures the ultrasound image inside her, a scrunched face on a tiny tennis ball head, bouncing and sloshing in the squishy gray, the little thing's home shaken like a snow globe. The baby probably hates tennis. Maria does not trip, but barely gets her racquet on the ball, just lifting it over the net.

"'Cheeseburger in Paradise' is shit," Julie says, "but some others are good."

Maria smartly stays at the net, and normally this would mean Doug should hit the ball at her so she can practice her angles, but this volley is not normal; it's like he's recognizing weakness and, with Julie's distractions, can't help himself from trying to beat Maria, win this point. If they were to play a whole match, he's certain now he could give her a run for her money. Instead of hitting the ball at her, Doug lofts a high arching lob over her head, believing she'll not even follow it, she'll just look at him, slouch her shoulders and tilt her head, calling him an asshole with every joint and muscle, but she turns and takes off, scrambling to get started, spinning her wheels like a cartoon character, before she barrels back to the baseline. He's certain now she's going to fall. She's going to fall, and it's his fault for playing the point, for trying to beat a pregnant woman. He *is* an asshole.

Julie sings, loudly again, "*I blew out my flip-flop, stepped on a pop-top.* That's pretty good, you've got to admit. Can't you just *see* that?"

Maria stumbles toward probably the best lob Doug has ever hit. With her back still turned to him, she flails at the ball and completely whiffs, whacking the racquet against her back and tumbling to the fence before catching herself from falling.

"People forget that song is so sad," Julie says.

Doug looks at his sister. He doesn't know why she's still talking about that stupid song when his pregnant wife has almost face planted on the hard court. She should stop. The point is over. "Are you okay?" he shouts to Maria.

Maria stands up straight, her back still turned. Doug sees her shoulders rise and fall, a deep breath. Maria is an avid practitioner of deep breaths before rash action. Doug wishes more people were like her in every way, lovers of animals, tolerant of family, mindful of heritage, connected physically and mentally, graceful, consciously taking the time to calm themselves with a deep breath before hurling their racquet against the fence or on the court, pausing thoughtfully before flipping birds, punching each other at bars, firing handguns into crowded porches, driving wildly to Chicago.

She traps the ball between her shoe and her racquet and kicks it up to her hand. When she turns around she's smiling. "Nice lob," she says and walks back to the baseline for her next serve. All the way across the court he can see a different intensity in her eyes. Maria tosses and serves.

His sister is still singing.

In the freezer they keep a bottle of vodka that hasn't been touched in a while. Doug prefers beer. He exchanges the tennis bag for a soft cooler and sticks the bottle in, searches the fridge for garnishes, a plastic yellow squeeze bottle of lemon juice in the shape of a lemon and some Tabasco. Brick looks at him like he can't believe he's left him in the condo all morning and is about to leave him again. He grabs Brick's leash and brings him along for company. At a corner bodega, Doug buys a bag of ice, plastic Solo cups, V-8 juice, and a sack of chili-roasted sunflower seeds to munch and spit if he has to wait. Maria and Julie decided to take a walk through the park. Because she hadn't given any indication she wanted to talk to Doug, he thought Julie might feel more comfortable confiding in Maria, woman to woman, so he left them alone. It's a beautiful day, he said. They should stay outside. He offered to meet them with Bloody Marys.

When Doug gets back to the court, Maria and Julie aren't there. He's not too worried. He figures they might take some time on their walk, Maria pointing out her favorite parts of the park while Julie finally unloads her pent-up confession. "The smell from the fritura trucks always makes me hungry"; *I'm having an affair*; "those old men will slap dominoes all day long"; *with a woman*; "look at the cute baseball players on their way to Little Cubs Field"; *who's also married*; "isn't it cool how the Puerto Rican flag sculpture spans the street like a welcoming gate?"; *to a violent meth addict*.

Doug still has no clue.

The courts are full. An older couple plays where Doug and Maria had been playing, each one of them decked out in full tennis whites like they're at Wimbledon. Doug sits down on the bench to watch and loops Brick's leash through the slats. He mixes a Bloody Mary—ice, vodka up to the first O in Solo, V-8, lemon squeeze, Tabasco. He pops chili-roasted seeds in his mouth one by one and watches the couple play. The heat of the seeds mixes perfectly with the V-8 and vodka. He makes a note to himself to rim a glass with chili powder next time he's mixing Bloody Marys at home. He gives Brick a couple of ice cubes to munch on. Watching the older couple makes Doug happy, both of them still active, still living in a city, still slowly but surely tapping the ball over the net to one another. He wants that to be he and Maria, still keeping the ball in play after all those years. Doug spits and drinks and laughs at himself for being so sentimental about these old people playing tennis. Sometimes he wishes he was more original. Chili powder on a Bloody Mary rim, he thinks—that might be original.

When the woman angles a winner way out of the old guy's reach, Brick chases the ball before he's snapped back by his leash. "40-love," the woman says. It sounds like a term of endearment. The old man picks up the ball a few feet away from Brick. Doug smiles at him, gives him a thumbs up.

"He ought to have a muzzle," the man says.

Brick stands with his leash taut, staring at the old man. Brick's harmless. Doug hates people who are scared for no reason, scared because they're ignorant, scared because they saw a special on *60 Minutes* that told them to be scared. Brick was chasing after a ball because that's what dogs do, not because he wanted to gnaw the old man's face off. Doug is more likely to gnaw the old man's face off. Doug stands up, spits shells, unties Brick. "You ought to have a forehand," he says, and takes Brick and his cooler outside the court, under the shade of a shedding cottonwood tree.

When he finishes his Bloody Mary and the women still aren't back, Doug ignores the screen telling him he's got four missed calls from "Dad" (Maxine) and looks up "Julie" on his cell phone, then presses the talk button. His call goes straight to voicemail. He knows Maria does not have her phone with her because it was in the tennis bag. It's not the smartest move but it has been almost an hour since he left them, and now he's worried and tired of waiting, so he and Brick set off looking for them. He walks all the way down to Division, stands on the corner for a minute or two, then turns around and walks all the way back, past the courts again, up to North Avenue. He doesn't see them anywhere. People must not have worried so much back in the days before cell phones. An unanswered phone simply meant you weren't at home, not dead in a ditch, not kidnapped, not randomly taking a road trip to Chicago. He thinks about Corey, calling and calling, worried sick until his kids told him where their mama was like it was obvious. That was pretty cold even for Julie.

Doug's close to the condo, so he decides to take back Brick along with the cooler that's getting too heavy. When he approaches the front door, he sees a piece of paper wedged between the buzzer and the front brick. It's Maria's scribble written on the back of a receipt. "We waited for you. Going shopping. Love Maria." Doug flips the receipt over. Julie bought a 64-ounce soft drink, a pickle, and a bag of pretzels at a Shell station in Bowling Green, Kentucky.

Julie thought Doug had said to meet him back at home. Maria couldn't remember what he'd said. After they'd taken a short walk through the park, they had gone to the condo looking for him and the Bloody Marys but couldn't get in. When he wasn't there and he didn't show up, they left. They'd taken a bus down to Wicker Park. Julie bought a pair of red cowboy boots at a vintage store. She treated Maria to lunch at a newly opened restaurant with an outdoor patio. They brought him back a hamburger and French fries.

"Why won't you answer your phone?" he asks Julie.

"I lost it," she says, swiping her hands across each other like she's finished, good riddance.

"There are still pay phones," Doug says. He realizes he sounds like Maxine.

He sits down at the counter in the kitchen and opens the Styrofoam clamshell holding his food. Maria is heating water up for tea. He doesn't blame her. It's easier to get mad at Julie. She sits next to Doug at the counter, his laptop open again. He can see she's checking her Facebook feed.

"You've done good," she says. "You can be whatever you want here."

"What do you want to be?"

"Maybe I'll move," Julie says. "I could be your nanny." She laughs and looks knowingly from the monitor to Maria. The kettle whistles and Maria pours the water into her mug. She grabs a magazine before walking back to the bedroom. She doesn't look at either of them.

Julie types something on the computer. Laughs. "Love or money?" Julie asks.

"Are those my only choices?" Doug bites into his burger. Mushroom Swiss. His favorite. Maria is good to him. He smells spaghetti but can't tell if it's something in the food, maybe the ketchup, the fries, or if it's coming from his sister.

"Apparently you can't have both," Julie says.

He figures this angle has something to do with why she's here. Doug thinks if you've ever been in love, have known what love feels like and means, the question is not even difficult. Of course, he and Maria aren't exactly flush with cash, so he hasn't really known the alternative. "Love," he says, his mouth full of juicy meat, cheese, and tender mushrooms. He hears the bathtub filling with water and wishes he was in there with Maria, her chamomile tea, her vanilla bubbles, her smooth belly poking through the suds-clouds.

"Okay," Julie says and closes the laptop.

For some reason Julie spends most of the afternoon in the guest bedroom. She comes out once and asks Doug for the phone. He hears her behind the closed door yelling at someone, probably Maxine. "He can't do that," she says. "Why is everyone on his side?" she says.

Doug presses Maria for any more information she might've gotten on their excursion, but Maria is being just as cryptic as Julie.

"She probably hates her kids," Maria says.

"What?"

"We didn't really talk about it."

Doug feels like he's in a sci-fi movie where everyone is in on a secret but him, the secret being that he's the alien, he's the foreigner, the planet he once ruled is being ruled by monkeys.

After Julie finally comes out of the bedroom, and after she takes another shower, and after she tries on a bunch of Maria's clothes to see what goes best with her new red boots, they head to a wine and beer bar at California and Augusta, one of Doug and Maria's favorite restaurants in the neighborhood, small plates so they can all share. They have to wait a little while for a table. Eating past nine o'clock and passing around mismatched plates of carefully crafted food makes Julie feel European, she says. Maria has a glass of red wine. Her doctor says it's okay, but Doug can't help looking around the restaurant to see who's noticing, who's whispering about the pregnant woman they think is knocking back glass after glass, who might be commenting on "her type" and casting false judgments about the future. When Doug looks around the restaurant, though, no one seems to be staring at Maria.

Toward the end of the meal, much to Doug's surprise, Maria tells him that he ought to take Julie to the honky-tonk down the street. When Julie bought those red boots, Maria had told her she knew just the place to wear them. The words honky-tonk get Julie excited. She squeezes Doug's arm, expressing her enthusiasm for the idea. Doug has never been to a honky-tonk down the street and has no idea how Maria knows about one. Someone at work must have told her. He pictures giant belt buckles, uncoordinated line dancing, ironed blue jeans, cowboy hats with feathers, a mechanical bull, but worst of all, country music. Where there are no real cowboys, there should not be a honky-tonk. As far as Doug knows, Chicago does not have real cowboys. Once the idea has been floated it's impossible to retract. Doug says they should all go home, that Brick needs to be let out, that he'll even turn on country music from the digital TV stations and Julie can line dance all she wants, in her boots, right there in the living room. While Doug pleads, Julie hands their waiter a credit card before either of them even notice. "Now you have to take me dancing," she tells Doug.

The three of them walk down the street together before Maria says she's getting a cab. Julie rubs Maria's belly, says bye, then disappears behind the red door of the bar. Once Julie's inside, part of Doug feels like getting in a cab with his wife and going home, leaving his phone with Julie so she can call for directions at closing time. It's not far. But Doug figures he ought to give it one more shot with his sister. Maybe she'll get drunk enough to tell him what the hell is going on in her life, provided the music isn't too loud.

He waits outside with Maria until a cab shows up. He tells her to text him when she gets home. She says she will.

A bar stretches most of the length of the right side of the honky-tonk. Doug sees only a few cowboy hats, no mechanical bull. At the far end of the bar, a small stage is set up for the band. They are not so loud he cannot still hear people talking and laughing. In front of the stage, couples dance together instead of in ill-formed lines. The music is whiny and twangy, but the place is all right, less of a costume party than he'd thought. Julie has found a booth to sit in and waves him over. The booth is filled with empties, brown beer bottles, short glasses with squeezed limes collapsed in puddles, cocktail straws scattered like branches.

"What'll you have?" Julie asks across the empties.

"Beer's good."

Doug reaches for his wallet, but Julie says she'll start a tab. As she walks to the bar, taller than most of the crowd in those boots, Doug catches men looking at her. After trying on most of Maria's closet, she ended up with a long-sleeved button up shirt, whose unbuttoned top three buttons allowed her the best opportunity to show herself off. Her shorts are the same too-short shorts she showed up in. Nobody should pair cowboy boots with shorts, but it's especially troubling on his sister. Doug sees a bearded man in a tight plaid shirt elbow his buddy when Julie squeezes next to him and leans over the bar. Doug is certain she sees the men looking at her but doesn't care. She would only care if they weren't looking at her.

She walks back carefully with a beer and a shot for Doug, a tall glass of something dark for herself. Doug smells grapes. "You happy?" he asks.

"As a clam," she says, pushing aside the empties with a swipe of her arm.

They clink glasses and Doug gulps the shot he didn't ask for but is grateful to have. Julie sucks on her small straw, swallows. "Remember NuGrape?" she asks.

He does. The grape soda they used to drink as kids, yellow can, bright purple letters. He has not seen a can of NuGrape in years. He wonders if they still make it. He laughs and nods.

Julie sucks on her straw again. "It's not NuGrape, but it's good." She pushes her drink across the table to Doug. The smell of grapes gets stronger. The drink is dark. He takes a sip. Grapes. Grapes and coconut.

Julie smiles. "It's called a Purple Martin. The only bar in Chicago with grape soda on the gun. Cowboy at the bar said so." Doug takes another sip of her drink, laughing at himself for thinking the grape smell came from her. She pulls the glass back from him. "Wanna dance?"

Doug does not like the idea of dancing with his sister. He tilts his beer back and shakes his head. "I'll be here," he says.

When Julie stands up to dance, he expects the men to descend on her like buzzards, but they don't. She dances by herself, spinning and twirling in a kind of hippie dance that doesn't fit the music. The only words Doug can make out coming from the baseball-capped singer are something about prison—just like every country song, he thinks—and the refrain, *Mama tried. Mama tried.* The dance floor is filled with couples, some of them same sex even, and he thinks about Maria's voicemail message from yesterday. He wishes she had stayed with them, had had it in her to come dance. He would take her out on the dance floor and have her faith in the future restored. Here are people dancing together, holding each other close, elbowing their buddies to check out good-looking women, listening to a live band playing real instruments, singing with real voices. Don't worry, Maria. See. Look around. Everything is going to be okay.

Doug checks his phone. No messages. Maria has not texted him yet. She should've been home already. She should've gotten in and already texted to say she was in. It's not far. He realizes they may lose the booth, but Doug steps outside to call her.

Smokers, laughing and talking, congregate away from the door. He'll tell Maria about them too. People still dance together. People still huddle together outside a bar and smoke together, even when they know they're killing themselves. Everywhere, people are still together with other people, socializing, having fun. She doesn't answer her cell phone. Her insistence that they keep a land line has never seemed necessary until now. A cell phone dies. A cell phone gets left on vibrate in a tennis bag. A home phone can ring and ring, wake anyone up. He calls the home phone, but she doesn't answer that either. Doug calls her cell again. Voicemail. Then back to the home phone letting it ring and ring until he hears his voice on the voicemail, "Hi. Doug and Maria can't—" he hangs up and redials the home phone. It rings four times before Maria finally answers. Doug unclenches his teeth. He did not know they were clenched.

"I was walking Brick," she says. She sounds funny, upset, maybe like she's lying. Doug thinks about the grape soda he just smelled, believing it was Julie. Deep down he has probably always known it wasn't true, that he didn't possess a telepathic sense for his sister's smell, but that hasn't stopped him from believing he did. He wishes he could use it on Maria, that he could smell her right now through the phone, tell what's wrong.

"I was worried," he says.

"I wouldn't do it," she says. "I swear I wouldn't."

She's crying now. Doug does not need to see her face or touch her tears to know. She is crying. All he smells is cigarette smoke.

"Maybe you didn't need that glass of wine." He jokes, but he knows he shouldn't joke.

"I wanted to fall today," she says. "When I was running for the ball, I wanted to fall. I wanted to trip on purpose. Right on my stomach." Now she is half laughing and half crying. "I wouldn't do it, but I wanted to."

Julie comes out of the front door looking for Doug. The bearded guy from the bar follows behind her. He is a full head shorter than her in those boots. He reaches into his front shirt pocket and fishes out two cigarettes, lighting one for Julie. They shake hands.

"We're coming home," Doug says.

"No," Maria says. "I'm okay. Stay with your sister."

When Julie sees Doug, she runs over and grabs him by the neck, hugging him tightly, smashing the phone between his ear, his hand, and her right breast. He can feel the cigarette burning next to his face, can smell coconuts and grapes from her breath. Maria says something else, something more, but he can't hear her now over his sister's singing.

Inside the Happiness Factory

I'm at an office birthday party when my phone jitters in my jeans. Casual Friday. I haven't had any cake yet, so I don't check my phone right away. I wait for my slice, patiently, watching each plate get passed to a coworker before I get mine — last, always last — red velvet cake with white cream cheese frosting, a plastic fork plunged, tines first, into the soft red sponge.

Along with the cake, the boss is passing out free tickets to The World of Coca-Cola, a short walk from our office building. Rewards for meeting our quarterly goals. "Good job. Excellence breeds excellence." Some people get two tickets, some three or four, some none. "It's really something else," the boss says to me. "If you've never been. Quite an experience."

I take my single ticket and my slice of cake. "Happy birthday, Teresa," I say cheerfully as I exit the break room.

The birthday girl doesn't look up from her Styrofoam cup of Diet Cherry Coke.

I take the cake to my cube and pull out my phone. The text is from a number I don't know, but it's not just a text, but a text and a picture of a baby, a cute blue-eyed baby girl with a red bow askew on her head. The baby is on her stomach on a red and white checkered picnic blanket spread over some short cut grass, using all her tiny baby muscles to lift up her neck. A spot of drool shines from the corner of her puckered baby mouth. This is all clearly a mistake.

The text: hey daddy

But I don't want it to be a mistake.

The baby is adorable, and I wish she really was mine, I was really hers, and this was a picture my wife took, my beautiful blue-eyed wife and my beautiful blue-eyed baby. We're at a picnic. My wife's toes peek through the blades of grass, long and slender toes, with nails painted the color of strawberry ice cream. And lots of other people are here with us at this picnic too, present with their own toes, family, sisters, friends, grandparents. And there I am, off camera, by the grill, flipping burgers and rolling hot dogs while the family *oohs* and *coos* over the baby. My wife stands there with her hands turned backwards at her waist, pushing her hips out like she used to when she was pregnant with our daughter. My wife wears a sundress, the one I bought her on our honeymoon to the Bahamas, and she turns her head over her tanned shoulder, and looks at me by the grill and says, "Ain't life sweet."

I call the number. No answer. I leave a message. "Hi, I got your picture. I'm not sure who you are, but your baby is beautiful. But unless you're looking for me, you probably have the wrong number. Maybe you are looking for me. If you are, you can call me back if you need to talk to me. Thanks."

Teresa's birthday cake tastes good.

The boss was right. The World of Coca-Cola really is quite an experience, like being inside a peppermint, swirls of red and white everywhere. In the lobby a white polar bear greets me and tries to shake my hand. In the bottling plant, robots deliver glass to conveyor belts where each bottle is cleaned and sanitized. The robots keep everything clean. In the tasting room I get to taste Coke products from all over the world to see what other drinks the Japanese might be enjoying. Our tastes aren't all that different. There's also a theater where they show a cartoon called *Inside the Happiness Factory*, all about what happens inside a vending machine once you slide in your money. All these little cartoon people scurry to work to deliver the ice-cold Coke to your hand. Each one gives a testimonial about their job, and it's funny, and it starts me thinking about how this is really an old idea, how we all used to think like this at some point when we were kids. At least I did. I used to think that for all the things that were too complicated to figure out, there were little people inside controlling the machinery. Inside a watch, tiny people move the gears around, syncing up time with the heavens, making sure you know where you need to be and when. And inside the TV, little people bring the shows to you, turning the channel when you want it, shining out all the bright colors that make up what you see. A camera, a car, a computer are all filled with little people, working together, making things go. And even inside the telephone, a crowd of them wait with tiny hammers to clang on a bell whenever someone wants to talk to you. You stop thinking this way eventually, about most things.

Chopsticks

When John and Angie got divorced, they did this thing where they sent out fake death certificates to all their friends. The certificates came in black envelopes and were printed in silver ink on black paper. Sophie thought this was clever. She's an artist.

"They didn't work together anyway," Sophie said.

In her mind, the act was justified because John and Angie recognized they were a rotten couple and found a creative way to show off their rottenness. I thought it was gross. I filed it away in my mental folder of "dumb stuff our friends do" and didn't think about it again until recently, until things soured for Sophie and me. They soured pretty quickly too, like, I don't know, like something you can imagine would sour quickly. Not to be outdone by our friends, Sophie said she wanted to have a party, a big party, where everyone got dressed up and celebrated the end of our marriage. I told her this was a bad idea, that I thought it was in poor taste.

"So suddenly you feel something," she said.

This is our problem, my problem. I no longer feel anything. I really don't. And thinking a divorce party is tasteless is not the same as feeling it. If I felt an emotion—anger, sadness, love, hate, loss, whatever—it would probably move me to act, to do something, but I don't feel anything, which is why I'm going along with it.

I woke up about nine months ago and looked at my wife still sleeping while the alarm was going off and I felt nothing. It wasn't like I was looking at a stranger. I knew who she was, the same person who'd been asleep on that pillow beside me for almost ten years, the same pouty lips, same wavy hair, same eyelids closed and spidered with faint purple veins, the same black tank top with its faded pink stars. The same ability to sleep through the alarm buzz. But I didn't feel anything. Not one ounce of love or passion or relief or comfort or solace or desire. Nothing. I turned off the alarm and took a shower to see if this was some kind of dream state, a fog that would lift in the hot water and fresh lather of soap and shampoo. But the shower didn't do anything for me, which was weird. Unlike a bath, which I can enjoy with another person, a shower has always been a solitary thing for me, a private act. A time to tune out the world. No music. No TV. Warm and alone. Just the echo of water splashing off the tiles and the soothing massage of the spray head. For me, the shower is sacred, a sanctuary almost, but that morning it was just a shower. There was water and soap and steam and a washcloth. Purely utilitarian. I toweled off and felt exactly the same.

Sophie was watching *Good Morning America*, her pillow doubled up under her head. She looked cute, but that was about all I could come up with. I got back in the bed with her and hugged her, buried my face in her neck to smell her hair and her sweet and sour morning skin. Not a thing.

"Tell me you love me," I said.

She laughed. We're not usually those kind of people. "I love George Stephanopoulos," she said.

"Just say it."

"I love you. I love you. I love you."

She might as well have said "I hate you," which I asked her to do next.

"I'm not going to say that."

"Please."

"Hate's not a joke."

I told her thanks and went and stood in front of the pantry and stared blankly at all the cereal boxes.

It got worse. Not worse, because with apathy there isn't really a scale, but more obvious. Nothing made me laugh. Or cry. I saw that commercial with Sarah McLachlan and her puppies and didn't even reach for a Kleenex. While I was jogging, not feeling winded or especially proud of my health, I witnessed a hit and run. I saw a biker get hit and the white car drive off and everything, but I didn't try to get the license number even though I probably had time to read it. I jogged in place as the crowd gathered, waiting for a feeling to hit me, sadness, rage, regret for not getting the license number, guilt for jogging in place like I couldn't even be bothered to stop moving, whatever, but I just idled on my toes, and when one of the witnesses asked me if I'd seen what happened, I shrugged.

Sophie said this was a classic case of depression, not to worry, we'd get through it together. She sent me to a doctor who asked me a bunch of questions about my parents. I answered with monosyllables and grunts. Sometimes I fell asleep. He prescribed me some pills that I eventually stopped taking because I couldn't ever remember to take them. So Sophie took them, and after a few weeks she said she'd never felt better in her life. I kept seeing the doctor so I could keep getting her pills. Bad idea. Her feeling good coincided with my not feeling a thing, and after several months of this, she said it was time we call it quits. She couldn't be with a man who didn't feel anything. I didn't refuse or cry or blame her, and it didn't hurt me when she said we were through, which probably made it all worse for her even though she tried to act like she didn't care either. She stuck out her hand for a shake like she'd just sold me a car.

And now we're at the party.

And now she cares.

Sophie's locked herself in the bathroom and won't come out. All the people she's invited are downstairs. I hesitate to call them our friends, because when I look at them, I don't feel friendship. Come, go, have a ball, have a heart attack, get drunk, act stupid, cheat on your spouse, drown in your alcoholism, so what? We should all feel ashamed. I cared about these people once, and here they are celebrating my divorce. I try to convince Sophie to come out, but she won't. She says she's not done yet. I don't know what she's doing.

"You're still flushing with number one," she says.

We have an eco-friendly toilet in our bathroom, an item she insisted on when we bought the condo. Sophie takes a lot of baths in our giant whirlpool tub, but she needed an eco-friendly toilet to conserve water. Two buttons: a large circular silver button for the liquid jobs and a smaller button set inside the larger button for the solid jobs. She accuses me of never knowing the difference.

"I hit the big button."

"Right. That's for number one, not for number two."

Sophie doesn't like to say the word "shit" when it's referring to what it really refers to. She'll use it artfully as an exclamation.

I've explained this to her before. How the buttons don't make sense. How if you're designing a toilet with two different flushes, logically, when more stuff is in the toilet you would push the button corresponding to the amount of stuff in the bowl. A lot to flush? Push the big button. But that's not how it works. Frequency is the design aesthetic with this toilet. Frequency of pushing. Right. And frequency has bred routine, which means I hit the wrong button even when I take a shit.

"Sorry," I say through the closed door, but I don't feel what sorry means. I jiggle the handle. Still locked.

"I need a plunger," she says.

There has always been a plunger in our bathroom. I guess she took this with her to her sister's house or figured prospective buyers would be turned off by a plunger hidden in a cabinet underneath the sink.

A crash comes from downstairs.

"Be right back," I tell her.

I head down to see what's going on, what's been broken. There's not much left to break. Sophie boxed up all the dishes and glasses and took them to the Salvation Army. She didn't want either one of us to have them. I bought one plate, one bowl, and one glass from Crate and Barrel. I should care if someone is down there in the kitchen breaking my one glass or one bowl or one plate, but I don't. I can buy more. I feel no kinship with these objects.

Everyone is dressed up as requested on the invitation, dark suits and black dresses. It looks like a funeral, except there's an abundance of catered appetizers spread all over the kitchen, a full bar manned by a kid in a black vest and bowtie, black balloons reaching for the ceiling. Everyone is drinking from black glasses. They must've been brought by the caterer.

Chalese is holding a large jagged piece of black glass. She's jabbing it at her husband Alan, who's scooting back and doing some evasive maneuvers like she's really trying to slice him. I don't wish she would or wish she wouldn't. More pieces of black glass are on the floor.

"Sorry," Chalese says when she sees me. She tosses the shard in an open trash bag, its red drawstring looped around a cabinet knob. "I'll clean it up," she says.

Chalese is sweet but annoying. She talks over you. She doesn't listen and tries to redirect every conversation and analyze every problem according to what she knows about. What she knows about is teaching kindergarten.

I tell her I don't have a broom.

She pulls her long dress up and gets down on all fours, using a napkin to brush all the pieces of glass into a pile. I am not concerned she will cut herself.

About a month ago, as we closed in on the reality of divorce, Sophie started doing things to try and hurt me, hurt me physically. "Can you feel me now?" she would ask, like that cell phone commercial, and burn me with a hot spatula. "Can you feel me now?" she would ask, and hit me as hard as she could in the kidney. I didn't see this as abuse. In some ways, I deserved it. I didn't get pissed or fly off the handle or retaliate or feel like I needed to. I felt pain on the surface—nowhere else.

Chalese picks up shards of glass one by one, pinched between her fingers, and drops them on the napkin. Her nails are painted black. Alan bends down to help. I watch.

"Where's Sophie?" Chalese asks, looking up at me from the floor.

Before I can answer, she's asking more questions.

"How's she feeling? Does she need my help?"

"She's upstairs."

"How are *you* feeling?" Alan asks.

Nobody knows for sure what our breakup is all about. Everyone assumes that Sophie and I drifted apart and the divorce is mutually agreed upon, amicable. I know they all speculate behind our backs, think that one of us is gay or one of us is impotent or barren, which would explain why we never had kids, but what we've told everyone is that this is just a timing thing, and our relationship has run its course, like, I don't know, a cruise or something.

I shrug.

They both give me looks like Sarah McLachlan's dogs.

Chalese stands up and shakes the napkin over the open trash bag. "I'm sorry," she says.

"It's not mine."

"Not about the glass." She grabs my arm and squeezes like I really have lost a loved one.

Alan stands up and pats me on the back and turns his lips in like he's trying to hold back tears. They feel this. They really do.

Mark has his phone plugged into a pair of portable computer speakers. He's made a special playlist for the occasion. Mark made a playlist for our wedding too—all of our favorite Elvis songs. Sophie and I love Elvis. Every bit of him, rock-a-billy beginning to fat carnival end. We danced to "It's Now or Never." Sophie thought this was funny. Thinking about Elvis now, our wedding, our song, should fill me with a wave of nostalgia, but it doesn't. What begins to play is funereal organ music, a dirge, then some Joy Division. *Love, love will tear us apart again.* Everyone's laughing and toasting.

"To love," Mark says. They all lift their black glasses.

I don't get it.

I head back upstairs to Sophie.

The door is open now.

She's standing over the toilet. She's wearing a sharp black dress shaped to the contour of her body. She cut all her hair off recently and has it slicked to her head, no more waves. She's looking very sci-fi. Heavily charcoaled eyelids, deep shades of sparkly silver on her cheeks, silver earrings the size of coasters. Her lips are dark purple. She's beautiful, an oddball kind of beautiful, and I can say this, objectively, and know it, because beauty is not a feeling. It prompts no corresponding reaction in my gut or heart or neck or balls or ankles or elbows or wherever I'm supposed to feel beauty. It's like I'm looking at one of her pieces. No, not art, something more soulless—an ad in a newspaper for Macy's, something you pass over on the way to somewhere else.

As I move closer to her, I see that the toilet bowl is full of toiletries. A Gillette Fusion Pro-glide razor, an Oral-B toothbrush and small tube of Crest Multicare toothpaste, Aveda Control Paste hair pomade, a bottle of Jack Black Silver Mark cologne, Optifree Replenish contact solution, a Lafont glasses case, and a stick of Dove Men +Care deodorant, fresh scent. Everything I was allowed to keep in the bathroom as long as I stashed it in a drawer so prospective buyers wouldn't see it and know someone was still living here. Sophie thought our condo would have a better chance of selling if it was empty. I had always heard the opposite. Nobody wants to buy an empty condo. People's imaginations are not sufficient to fill the space with their own stuff. They want to see your things, judge you for your poor taste, tell the realtor how they could do better. But Sophie insisted on emptying our place out. I went along. I didn't care. I've been sleeping on an air mattress in our bedroom. Every morning I deflate it and put it back in a bag and place it on a shelf in the master closet where I'm still allowed to keep some clothes as long as they're hung neatly. This should be depressing. Living in the empty condo we shared together, our first, sleeping on the floor without my wife, her living with her sister and her family out in the suburbs. Who wouldn't feel this?

The sight of all my toiletries in the bowl doesn't register as my toiletries in the bowl. It's just a bunch of stuff.

"That's why it's clogged," I say.

Sophie pulls a reel of toilet paper off the spool, pulls and pulls and pulls, then wraps it around her hand until it's a sufficiently-sized ball and tosses it in the toilet. She hits the smaller button on top of the tank, the button for number two. The toothpaste chases the toothbrush around the bowl. The wadded toilet paper unfurls and disintegrates in the swirling water. I grab Sophie by the arm and pull her away from the overflow.

"Do you remember our first night here?" she asks.

Sophie keeps bringing up stuff from our past, hoping a fond memory will knock me back to my senses.

"I don't have amnesia," I tell her.

"We ordered noodles and ate in the bathtub."

"Your idea."

"The smell of the food made me feel like soup. Like we were in a bath of broth and at any second God could pluck us out with his giant chopsticks."

For a second, a flicker of feeling pulses through me. *Chopsticks*. When she says *chopsticks*. Not the bath or the noodles or the silly image of God as a bearded old man using wooden utensils or the memory of us here in our first place together, but just the word itself. Then it's gone.

"Say that word again."

"What word?"

"Chopsticks." I feel nothing when I say it.

"Chopsticks," she says.

A thrilling shiver, like somebody's lightly running their fingers along the back of my neck. It's not totally pleasant, but it's something. I don't have any idea why.

Sophie slaps me hard across the cheek. "I feel better now," she says. She hooks her arm through my arm and we walk down the stairs together.

Mark has cued up Elvis's "Amazing Grace." People are crying. For real. Once Sophie sees our friends and hears The King, she starts too.

So much for feeling better.

I see the tears cutting streams down her silver cheeks, the dark eye makeup melting, and I should feel like this is all wrong, that what we are doing is wrong, that what Sophie has done with all this is try to take me to the brink so I would snap out of my funk, and now we are at the brink and I'm not snapping, not waking, and she's realizing this, and it's all going to be over soon, and she really doesn't want it to be, and now she's crying because "Amazing Grace" is playing and all our friends are here dressed in black and it's just like somebody is dying.

But I don't care.

Chalese hugs Sophie and hands her a black glass full of wine. She wipes the side of her hand on Sophie's cheek, smearing the tears, then looks at me like I'm a monster because I'm not crying, like this is the first time she's realized what is really going on here. The odd girl in her kindergarten is getting bullied. That's how I'm sure Chalese understands this.

I open the drawer where we kept our silverware and where I've been piling takeout packages of plastic forks and knives and spoons and chopsticks since Sophie moved. I take out a pair of chopsticks and unsheathe them from their red paper package, snap them apart at the end where they're joined and roll them in my fingers. The same feeling from upstairs is not here. I read the package. On one side is a brief history of the chopstick as a utensil, thousands of years old. On the other side, instructions on how to use them. Sophie and I never needed instructions. I position a pair of chopsticks in my fingers and pick a shrimp off a platter and pop it in my mouth. Again nothing.

Alan is watching me. "You've lost it, buddy."

"Say the word *chopsticks*."

"Chopsticks."

A flush of pain and pleasure, like someone is cleaning out my ears with a Q-tip but digs too deep. It lasts longer this time, maybe because when Alan says the word he sustains the S, something that would usually annoy the hell out of me about Alan. I suppose I could walk around all the time asking people to say the word *chopsticks*. Can I love my wife again if all she ever says to me ends with the word *chopsticks*? We need spreadable butter from the store, *chopsticks*. Hand me the remote, *chopsticks*. Will you rub my back, *chopsticks*? I could change my name.

I take out the other red packages in the drawer and remove all the chopsticks, but don't break them apart. I arrange the sticks on the counter, stack them, pick them up and drop them, make shapes with them, stick them over my ears like pencils.

Alan walks away cautiously.

I feel the urge to get that feeling back, and this in itself is a feeling, so the fact that I'm putting in an effort to find out what's so special about chopsticks means I care. I care about getting the fleeting feeling back that comes from a word, no matter how fleeting the feeling. This is something.

Sophie comes over and puts her hand on my shoulder. She notices all the loose sticks and packages. "You remember that toaster we had that was too deep for English muffins?" she asks. "They wouldn't pop up all the way so we had to dig them out."

"Yeah. What did we use?"

She pulls the chopsticks off my ears, says the word.

I feel my balls clinch.

She can tell something's going on. "What's up with chopsticks?"

Every hair on my body stands up.

She whispers in my ear. "Chopsticks."

I'm in love with her again. I kiss her.

But then it's gone.

It's like kissing a wall.

"Be right back," I tell her.

The noodle place is three blocks away on the corner.

I used to love the smell here, ginger and chili oil and garlic and broth. Not now. It doesn't stink, but it doesn't smell appetizing either. I take a seat and order a bowl of tom kha gai soup. I love this soup. I always order it. I've even ordered it since this happened to me, sitting at our condo, alone on the air mattress, my computer open in front of me watching reruns of *Seinfeld*, and it gave me nothing. I didn't laugh. I didn't feel warm or satisfied. I didn't feel sad or lonely or empty. But sitting here now, I really want to love this soup again.

A couple sits next to me at a table for two. He's eating pad thai and she's eating what looks like spicy basil noodles. He's using a fork. She's using chopsticks. Her hair is in pigtails and she wears pink thick-rimmed glasses. He's in a baseball cap and a sweatshirt. They're young, but probably not as young as they look because they're both drinking beer. Both of their cellphones are on the table and he picks his up every now and then out of habit when there's a lull in the conversation. At the edge of their table, a tall glass holds a bouquet of chopsticks housed in their red packages. Before I even know what I'm doing or why I'm doing it, I reach over and pull one out. I slip the pair from the sleeve and break the sticks apart at the end, then rub them together. I place them across the rim of the boy's bowl of noodles.

I can tell what he's thinking. His look says it all. He's thinking he doesn't know how to use chopsticks, and that's why he's using a fork, and it's less embarrassing than trying to do something he's not used to, something hard, something that may take some practice, something that may have him looking foolish, especially in front of this girl.

"Are you the chopsticks Gestapo?" he asks.

When he says the word, my ears get hot.

The girl laughs at his joke. "It tells you how," she says and picks up her empty chopsticks package. She pushes her glasses up on her nose and reads. "Tuck under thumb and hold firmly."

She reaches across the table to grab the boy's hand, placing one chopstick in the web of skin between his thumb and forefinger. "Add second chopstick. Hold it as you hold a pencil."

She helps him with the other stick and continues to read. "Hold first chopstick in original position. Move second chopstick up and down."

Every time she says the word I feel like I could cry. My nose buzzes. My throat and eyes itch. My stomach drops. I want her to keep reading forever, but there are so few instructions.

"Now you can pick up anything," she reads.

The boy tries, pinching at the air awkwardly. He pokes the chopsticks into his pad thai and fumbles them all over his noodles. He laughs and repositions the chopsticks, trying again.

Piss-ants

Skip knocked on the cabin door. Didn't get an answer. Walked right in. The place was as he remembered it. Stuffed with stuffed animals. Birds and foxes on fake wood perches. Deer heads hovering over the wood-burning stove. Largemouth bass in exaggerated poses of high drama. A stink hung in the air like a chandelier. It was Martin.

He was in front of the TV. But the TV wasn't on. He was leaned back in a recliner, his hair spread out long and greasy around his balding head like a funky halo. He had a beard now.

"Janet wants you home," Skip said.

Martin looked at him and smiled. "I am home." His teeth gleamed. Those perfectly straight, perfectly white, perfectly perfect teeth, alabaster marvels in the midst of his foulness. White as china. White as paper. White as Sherwin-Williams high gloss. If he'd spent less money on those goddamned teeth, maybe he wouldn't be in this mess.

"You don't get to just leave," Skip said.

"It's not the life I want."

"You chose it."

"It doesn't fit me anymore." Martin snapped down the recliner. Tossed his hair back like a fashion model. He scooped two dripping cold beers out of a white Styrofoam cooler and went foraging around in a sideboard cabinet until he found two familiar koozies decaled with pictures of pheasants in mid-flight. They'd always called them *piss-ants*. A joke they used to think was funny once upon a time. Martin slid the beer cans into the twin koozies. Twirled them in his palms like revolvers. Gave a *follow-me* motion with his head.

Outside they knocked dead leaves and pecan husks from lawn chairs and sat on the deck. A small hill led down to the fishing pond where Skip had caught his first fish, gigged his first frog, met his first cottonmouth. Martin spread out his arms and helicoptered his torso from side to side. "Make me an offer."

"With the trees?"

"No. Without the trees. Of course with the trees, dummy."

"I don't have any money."

"Let's pretend."

"Five an acre."

"Sold." Martin looked down at the deck planks and picked up two loaded pecan shells nestled in a seam. He squeezed them until one cracked against the other. Flecked off the tiny armor plates of shell with his thumb to get to the nut. Martin claimed his daddy used to sit in blinds and shoot BB guns at the poor folks trying to steal all his yard nuts.

"Want to go fishing?" Martin asked. He chewed the pecan in his glowing teeth.

Of course Skip wanted to go fishing.

Martin had a johnboat with a trolling motor, and they puttered around in the pond searching for the big one until it got dark. Martin said he had some quail in the freezer and would love it if Skip stayed for supper. So Skip stayed for supper, and they emptied a box of grits into a big black pot, threw in some cream cheese, and wrapped the quail in bacon before slapping them on the grill. They sat on the deck and drank beer and nibbled all the meat off those tiny bird bones and dug their spoons directly into the black pot of cheese grits. Late in the night, Skip's cell phone started vibrating. It was Janet. She kept calling and calling. So Skip shut it off.

The next morning Skip woke up with a powerful headache. He walked out on the deck and saw Martin in the pond, naked, the water just below his hips.

"Come on in," Martin shouted.

"I'm good."

"You've never been good at anything."

Maybe a dip would help his head. He stripped to his briefs and ran down to the pond, cannonballed off the dock into the surprisingly warm autumn water.

When he came up, a wet piece of mud slapped him in the face. Martin had hurled a wad of sludge at him. He turned around to show Skip his back.

"Get my back."

A mud bath. Maybe that explained his stink.

Skip plunged his hand into the sludgy pond floor and shoveled up a clump of muck. Hurled it at Martin. He arched his back and let out a howl. So Skip did it again. Soon they were both spackled with mud. They laid out on the dock, far enough away from each other as to not feel queer, and let the mud calcify into a crusty skin.

Soon Skip felt shade darken his closed eyelids and a coolness settle on him, like a heavy cloud moving over the sun. He opened his eyes. Martin loomed over him in all his naked mud-striped glory.

"You want Janet?" he asked.

"Pardon?"

"There's no shame in it."

"I don't know what you're talking about."

"You don't think I appreciate what I've got. You don't think I know how good I have it."

"I'm just the messenger."

"Want me to shoot you?"

"Not particularly." Martin nudged Skip with his big toe. "You give up too easy. Like always."

Martin jumped off the dock, turning a goofy somersault into the water. He stayed under for a long time. Skip wondered if he'd hurt himself. Landed on an unseen stump and broke his neck. But soon he was back again, spitting nasty pond water into the morning air.

Skip borrowed a pair of Martin's dry boxers — clean ones, he promised — and they went fishing again. But it wasn't the same.

Just before dark Skip said he had to head back. They stood outside Skip's car with the door open. Martin put a hand on Skip's shoulder and squeezed. "We do the best we can with what we've got," he said.

But Skip knew he could do better, so he balled up his fist and popped Martin right in the nose, stunned him with a jab. Martin blinked and wobbled on his heels. Sneezed. Laughed. Teeth shining. If he hadn't laughed, that might've been the end of it. But he'd always thought too little of Skip. He tried to hit him again, but Martin ducked and took off running. Skip chased him around the side of the cabin. At one time Martin had been faster. Not today. Not anymore. Skip caught him by the back of his shirt and pulled him down in a horse-collar tackle. Martin cackled like a lunatic, making everything worse.

"Stop laughing," Skip said.

He didn't.

So Skip grabbed a wet wedge of wood from the woodpile pyramid and cracked Martin square in his teeth, knocked a nugget clear out of his mouth. That got his attention, but still he kept laughing. So Skip hit him with the wood until he stopped.

▼▼▼

Janet answered her door in a long men's robe, red and black plaid. She wore ratty fur slippers on her feet, matted and gray, the fur sticking together in spots like a wet rabbit. She shuffled into the kitchen and Skip followed. The robe covered her whole body, not even a bare ankle to admire. It must've been Martin's. He'd hoped she'd be wearing a sports bra. Yoga pants at least.

She sat down at their kitchen table, a long piece of reclaimed wood, like something from a shipwreck. He'd left Martin in the back of the car, but he wasn't ready to tell her that just yet.

"Can I get a beer?"

She waved a limp arm at the fridge, help yourself.

Skip found a brown bottle hiding behind a gallon of soy milk, the same shit-ass beer they'd been drinking at the cabin. He twisted the cap and swigged.

"What did he say?"

Skip kept the bottle to his lips.

"What did he say, Skip?"

Skip drank slowly, curling the cold beer around his cheek and tongue, warming it, bubbling it up until it stung and he had to swallow. He leaned against the concrete countertop and took another swig. Janet had started the dishwasher before he'd gotten there and it was wooshing warm air against his leg. The kids had crude pictures they'd drawn and colored pinned on a bulletin board on the pantry door, and under a yellow thumb tack was a picture of Janet and Martin with backpacks on, both of them smiling like they'd saved the world by taking a hike.

"I've got to pee," he said. He set his beer on the countertop and hurried down the hallway toward the master bedroom and bath. He knew the way. He turned on the shower. Felt the white, fluffy towels hanging on their respective hooks. Smelled the lotions they kept on either side of their dual vanity. He took off his clothes and stood in front of the fogging mirror in his friend's boxers. Martin's toothbrush would be the dry one.

It Don't Get No Better Than This

The ball wasn't even hit all that hard, the ball the Colonel hit, the ball that Peeps saw looping over his head into left-centerfield as he took off for third base, keeping his eyes on Coach Ross who was side-skipping down the base line, not giving him a signal yet, not a hold, not a wave, nothing. Peeps was sure he'd put up the stop sign. He could feel himself slowing down, already coasting, anticipating Coach Ross throwing up two hands like he was trying to keep a wall from collapsing. But he didn't. Peeps was shocked. One of the outfielders must've dropped the ball, booted it, but he couldn't turn around to look. He was going home.

He cut a sharp turn at third like he'd been taught and dug in hard, his short legs churning toward the plate. The catcher sized him up, pumped his fist into his mitt, readying for the throw. Peeps still didn't look back. The crowd was silent, or seemed silent, either that or something was clogging his ears: pumping blood, a surge of adrenaline, loose foam from his batting helmet. He was slow. Jesus, he was slow. Like he was running in place, just like all his teammates said, like Fred Flintstone, his legs spinning without moving anywhere, kicking up dirt before finally gaining traction. Now Fred Flintstone was plodding down the third base line trying to score the winning run in the state championship game. He saw the catcher sink lower in his crouch, pump his fist into his mitt one more time and take a small step back, grinding his spikes in the dirt. The throw was coming. Inside. Peeps would have to slide on the inside, the only part of the plate the catcher didn't have covered. His ears opened and he heard the crowd screaming and his teammates yelling, "Get down! Get down!" and something else, another voice, a small one, one between his ears, one that sounded like someone he knew, a dumb redneck saying some dumb redneck things.

Earlier that day, before the game, in the locker room, Coach Ross told the team he had a special guest who wanted to share a few inspirational words with them. Peeps thought it might be somebody famous here to wish them all good luck, maybe an ex-Brave like Tom Glavine or maybe even Dale Murphy, but Peeps was disappointed when he saw it was just Mitch Crandall. Mitch had been on the last Charity Christian Academy baseball team to win a state championship, almost twenty years ago. Since then Mitch had gone on to become a raging meth head turned born-again youth minister, but the worst kind of youth minister, the kind that didn't get paid for the job, the kind that spent all his free time organizing Bible study groups and prayer breakfasts and sing-alongs so he could hang out with kids half his age. After regaling the current team with stories of his glory days and leading them in a ridiculously long prayer that managed to thank everyone from Jesus to the school cafeteria staff, Mitch ended with this: "Win or lose," he said, "it don't get no better than this."

And this pearl of redneck wisdom was what Peeps could not get out of his head when he slid, headfirst, barrel rolled really, tumbling in front of the plate with his right arm extended, trying to keep his body away from the tag as the catcher caught the throw and lunged for Peeps whose gloved fingertips barely nicked the black border of the plate, safely scoring the winning run. *It don't get no better than this.* While stuck at the bottom of a suffocating scrum of sunflower seed spit and Gatorade breath and stale Bazooka Joe and clandestine dip and sweat and leather and farts. *It don't get no better than this.* While shaking hands with the losers of Pruett Presbyterian, while holding the enormous trophy in his arms and managing a weak smile, while hugging all his teammates and friends and seeing his parents clapping in the stands. *It don't get no better than this.* But as great as this was, as great as winning the state championship was, Peeps wasn't feeling it. Of course it got better than this. Didn't it?

Peeps sat on the bench in front of his locker in his socks and sliding pants, staring at the puddle of his uniform on the worn floor. 21. The last time he'd ever put it on. Next year the number would be somebody else's. He wondered if the school might retire it. He'd scored the winning run and ended the twenty year drought of CCA championships. That was worth something.

There'd be a trophy in the trophy case and that would be nice.

Move on. Don't be such a Mitch.

Peeps found a Snickers in his locker, unwrapped it, and took three quick bites.

The Colonel, freshly showered with a towel around his waist, sat on the bench next to him. "What time's everybody getting there?"

"Whenever."

There was a party at Peeps' tonight. His parents had set it up. They wanted to have all his friends over and let them celebrate a great season even if they'd ended up losing. These parties usually got pretty big.

"Shannon's coming," the Colonel said. "She wants to hook up with you."

"I thought she was on a cruise."

"She's back. Told me she wants to send you out with a bang."

"Nice try."

The Colonel shrugged and sprayed down his whole body with an aerosol that smelled like a field of fermented strawberries and buttholes. He placed two blue ice packs on either side of his left bicep, squeezing one between his arm and ribs and holding the other with his right hand. This was the postgame routine. Peeps would wrap an Ace bandage around and around the ice packs, securing them to the Colonel's powerful left arm to freeze the pain. This was the last time he'd do it. The Colonel was a junior. He'd be back. Peeps didn't want to get all sentimental. He didn't want to say something like *who's going to do this when I'm gone?* or *I'll bet you'll miss me* or some other crap like that. The truth was everyone would be fine. This was what people like Mitch didn't get. Somebody else would have Peeps' locker and his number and would wrap the Colonel's arm and would call pitches for him and he would deliver them with the velocity he was known for. The Colonel had told Peeps that he was the best who'd ever caught him, that when he was on the mound throwing to Peeps he felt like he could put the ball wherever he wanted, that it felt totally comfortable, like he was playing catch, and he couldn't explain it. He was glad the Colonel had told him all that, but now it was over. They both knew it as he wrapped the Ace bandage around the Colonel's arm, but neither one of them needed to say anything. So they didn't. Peeps hooked the small metal teeth in the stretchy fabric to keep the bandage secure. The Colonel patted him on the shoulder. And that was that.

At home, Peeps showered and jacked off to thoughts of Shannon in nothing but her knee-high softball socks. He put on khaki shorts and a black and gray bowling shirt with his nickname woven on the chest and was just getting ready to sit by the pool and relax when his dad sent him out to get ice for the party. *Can't rest on your laurels, Hoss.* Then what do you call what you're doing next to a 54 quart Igloo cooler filled with cold beer, Dad? Peeps would not come back to Charity and turn into his father. His brother could, but not him.

There were two exits in Charity, the nice exit and the dirty exit. The nice exit had a Red Lobster and the Mexican restaurant Dos Marcos and a Chick-fil-A and gas stations with clean restrooms, full-service diners, groceries, and soft-cloth automatic car washes. The dirty exit had cheap motels and pawn shops, a ShrimpShack, a Chinese buffet, liquor stores full of fifths and forties, pay before you pump gas stations. Driving north on I-75, if you stopped at the first Charity exit for gas and a pee break only to discover that two miles farther was another exit with flowers planted in the medians and hotel chains with names you'd recognize, you would curse yourself for not waiting for all the better options. Peeps' house was six miles outside the city limits, closest to the nice exit, where he could use his dad's Chevron card at Sid's.

Peeps leaned against his truck as it filled up and stared at the silver ice chest decorated with a grinning Eskimo kissing another grinning Eskimo in the way they're supposed to. A payphone stood next to the ice chest, a phone book dangling from a chain. He could call him. He could call him and talk to him, ask him what the heck he meant, tell him he disagreed. Maybe then he could get the stupid quote out of his head and stop feeling like crap and start feeling like a party. Peeps looked him up: Mitchell Crandall. No listing. Mr. and Mrs. Richard Crandall were listed, Rick and Mary, Mitch's parents. They'd taught Peeps Sunday school in fifth grade.

He pulled out his cell and dialed the number.

A woman answered. "Hello?"

"Is Mitch in?"

"Mitch doesn't live here anymore. May I ask who's calling?"

"It's Ben Salley. I was just—"

"Congratulations, Ben! We were at the game today. Nice slide. Mitch was there. Did you see him?"

"Yes, ma'am," Peeps answered. "He gave a nice prayer."

"I don't know where he got off to. He'd love to hear from you. Let me give you his cell."

He heard her set the phone down, drawers opening and shutting, her hollering for Mr. Rick. There were some in town who thought Mitch got a little too friendly with a few of the flock from his youth group, a little too touchy. Peeps didn't know if this was true and didn't want to think about it. No matter how friendly Mitch was, it always seemed fake to Peeps.

Mitch's mom gave him the number. "Funny how we don't know anybody's numbers anymore," she said. "Everything's in our little devices. I guess our brains'll just turn to grits."

Peeps told her thanks and called Mitch's cell. No answer. Not even a voicemail greeting, but Peeps let the phone keep ringing. For some reason he couldn't hang up.

A few people drove by Sid's Chevron and saw him standing next to his truck, recognizing it from the CCA baseball sticker on the tailgate, a huge white baseball with red stitching, the school's letters entwined in an Old English font. They honked. This was Charity: horns honking when you're just trying to fill your tank or make a phone call, eyes combing over your drugstore purchases at checkout to see if you bought condoms, peeking at your ATM receipt to check your balance, the casual flip of a hand over the steering wheel, a wave from a complete stranger. Peeps never got this. A total stranger saying "hey" from his passing vehicle, somebody just waving, just acknowledging your mutual existence. You could be a child rapist, a murderer, somebody leaving a wake of hate and evil. Why would anybody wave to somebody he didn't know?

Peeps wouldn't.

The gas nozzle clicked. He went inside to add four bags of ice to his total.

Sometimes Mitch hung out at Dos Marcos and read his well-worn and abundantly flagged Bible while he drank Sprite with lime wedges, lots of lime wedges, piled up in a plastic bowl usually used for salsa. A lot of people in town went to Dos Marcos because other than the Red Lobster there weren't that many places for a decent night out. Peeps figured Mitch went there because he liked to be seen reading his Bible in public. Or maybe he just liked the creamy white cheese dip like everyone else.

Peeps looked around the restaurant for Mitch. The donkey piñata swayed in the breeze from an air conditioner vent. A Mexican soap played on the TV hung high in the corner of the room, or something that looked like what he thought a Mexican soap looked like, lots of boobs and mustaches. A horse.

He didn't see Mitch anywhere.

Peeps was about to leave when Kelli came in with the rest of the Cooper clan—her parents Mr. Jim and Miss Ann and her little sister, Kelsey, minus the Colonel, who was probably already over at Peeps'. All the Cooper kids' names started with a *K*, but Keith was the only one with *F* for a middle initial. KFC. The Colonel.

"Congrats," Kelli said and hip-checked him against the front counter. "You played well today, Ben." Kelli wouldn't call him by his nickname, not anymore.

She had on a peach-colored Polo shirt and mommish-looking white capri pants, her hair in a high ponytail like when she pitched. Peeps loved to watch her pitch just like he loved to catch for her brother. They were twins, and their bodies were built the same, tall and lanky, clumsy except when they were on the mound or in the circle where they seemed to belong. She was wearing pointy old-lady glasses with a gold chain looped from the frames. In class she wore glasses, but that was the only time he'd seen her in them, and they weren't ugly ones like these. She and her brother didn't resemble each other that much in the face, but for some reason, tonight she looked more like him.

"Join us, Peeps," Mr. Jim said as he wrapped a strong arm around Peeps' shoulder and guided him to their usual table.

The waiter came and took their orders. Peeps said he wasn't hungry, so he just got a Mountain Dew. Kelli ordered a quesadilla. "I made something for you," she said. She unfolded a piece of paper from her pocket and gave it to Peeps. They shared a table in art class. She'd drawn a pencil sketch of him getting ready to gun down a would-be base stealer. Except it wasn't so much him as it was a muscled-up cartoon version of him. He looked brave and strong, his over-sized arm cocked near his ear like he'd been taught, capitalizing on every second. A catcher had to be quick. Quick was different than fast. Peeps could improve his quickness with good technique, proper footwork, snapping his arm straight to his ear and whipping the ball down to second, all in one move, no wasted motion. She'd drawn muscles where muscles didn't exist. Number 21 was taut across the exaggerated V-shape of his back. Peeps was not shaped in a V. Instead of a ball he was holding a bolt of lightning like he was about to unleash a serious storm on second base. Underneath the cartoon image she'd pasted a Bible verse, the letters and words cut from magazine ads like an inspirational ransom note: "That is why, for Christ's sake, I delight in weaknesses, in insults, in hardships, in persecutions, in difficulties. For when I am weak, then I am strong. 2 Corinthians 12:10"

He couldn't tell if she was calling him weak or strong, but he liked the picture.

"I don't really look like this."

Kelli grabbed the drawing from him. "Ungrateful."

He snatched it back. "I like it." He folded it quickly and stashed it in his pocket.

"I don't know what Keith'll do without you next year," Mr. Jim said. He shook extra salt over the already salted tortilla chips until Miss Ann took the shaker from him. "You know that kid that looks like a possum—"

"Jim!"

"What? He does. That kid looks just like a possum. What's his name?"

"Possum," Peeps said. He saw Kelli roll her eyes.

"See." Mr. Jim shot Peeps a finger pistol. "This Possum can't catch him like you."

167

"You know who else looks like a possum?" Miss Ann asked. "George Jones. The country singer. They call him that, don't they? The possum."

"They did," Mr. Jim said. "He's dead now."

"His name is Edward Goode," Kelli said.

"Good. Bad. He can't catch Keith," Mr. Jim said. "I'm worried."

"He'll be all right," Peeps said. He grabbed his Mountain Dew and stood up from the table, snagged a chip and crunched. "Better get to my party. Y'all have a good night," he said and started to walk away until he saw Kelli poking out her bottom lip in an exaggerated pouty face.

She'd be better than Mitch. Mitch was a dead end. Hopeless. Even if he found him, what would he say? "Hey man, I think it does get better than this." Mitch would laugh, want to debate, ask Peeps to get down on a knee and hold his hand and pray with him. This would lead nowhere. He didn't know where Kelli would lead either, but she'd be better than Mitch.

"Wanna come?" he asked.

Kelli shook her head. "Not my scene."

Of course not. Peeps looked to Mr. Jim and Miss Ann for some help. Didn't they think Kelli deserved a night out, could use one? They both looked down into their drinks. Kelsey had cheese dip on her mouth. The family wasn't getting into it.

"I need your help," he said.

"With what?"

"Some art."

He knew she wouldn't believe him, none of them would, but it was all he had. What she liked was art, and what he wasn't good at was art, and what they shared was a table in art. It was logical.

The waiter brought their food. Dos Marcos was the fastest place in town, like they already had every popular platter assembled and basking under heat lamps just waiting for someone to order the number 7, the number 14, the Speedy Gonzalez combo.

"I'll take mine to go," Kelli said.

On their way out Peeps paid his check at the front counter and dropped a quarter in the plastic box for a couple of packets of Canel's Mexican gum—one green, one white. Kelli's food smelled up his truck, so he rolled the windows down. He thought she might eat it quickly so they could throw the box away before they went anywhere, but she put it in the floorboard between her sandaled feet like she was going to save it for later. The peach color of her toenails matched the peach color of her shirt, matched her fingernails, matched her lipstick.

Kelli hadn't always been like this.

Growing up she was one of them, hanging out with her brother and his friends. They were all close. They did everything together, never cutting her any slack, not easing up on her because she was a girl. All the boys took credit for how good an athlete she turned out to be. But her freshman year she went loopy. Most kids rebelled against their parents; Kelli rebelled against her twin. She tried to be everything her brother wasn't. She stopped playing sports. She stopped studying. She got caught smoking at school. She got suspended and when she came back, she roamed the halls getting into fights with teachers. Everyone assumed she was on drugs. Some people claimed that Coach Gregg had gotten her pregnant and she had to have an abortion and that's why she went nuts. They kicked her out of CCA and she had to go to the public school for a while. Eventually Kelli got things straight. She re-dedicated her life to God, stopped the Goth girl stuff, and was allowed back. But when she was gone, still wearing black and self-piercing, she'd ridden her bike down a two lane highway not built for bicycles all the way out to Peeps'. She said she wanted to go swimming. Cool with Peeps. He was going into his junior year at the time. She should've been going into her sophomore year, but everything she did kept her back. Peeps' brother was there, fishing by the pond. His mom was at the grocery store. It was like Kelli knew exactly when to come. They swam. She laid out in a lounge chair in a black bikini. She hardly had any boobs, but he could see the outline of her nipples sucked to the wet black fabric. She said she was thirsty and went inside while Peeps sat outside and watched his brother fish. She didn't come back. After a while he went in to check on her. He didn't really know her anymore and didn't know what she could be up to, but he figured it might be something bad. He walked into his bedroom and heard the shower running behind the half-closed bathroom door. If she was in there, she'd know he used Head and Shoulders. He wondered if he'd left his dirty underwear on the floor. He called her name, "Kelli." She didn't answer. He called again. Nothing. Nobody could've taken a shower for that long. He pushed the door open and peeked in, not wanting her to think he was a perv. The bathroom was steamy, and he couldn't make out anything behind the frosted sliding glass doors of the shower. He took another step before he was able to see the silhouette of her body lying in the tub. At first he thought she'd killed herself in his bathroom, slit her wrists and bled out in his tub, something he'd never get over, but he didn't see any blood, nothing tinted pink behind the glass. He knocked on the outside of the doors. "Kelli?"

Her laugh scared him, sort of like a giggle but not totally a giggle, something new, a laugh he'd never heard before and hadn't heard since. "Yes."

"What are you doing?"

She slid the glass door open. The water pelted her body from the spray head. She was still in her bikini, her skin slick and shiny, her dyed black hair wet and worming over her face. She had her left hand between her legs, under the waistband of her suit bottom.

"Is this a sin?" she asked.

After that things got even weirder.

Peeps started the truck and cranked the A/C. He asked her what she'd ordered even though he'd heard her order it. Now that they were in the truck together he had no idea what to do with her.

"Quesadilla."

"Are you gonna eat it?"

"You want it?"

He could find room for a quesadilla, but he probably didn't need a quesadilla. "Just wondering."

"Why are we sitting here?"

"Where do you want to go?"

"I don't know. You need my help or something."

"Right. Art."

"Uh-huh. Art."

Kelli bent over and picked up her Styrofoam to-go box and opened up the lid. She dipped a triangle of quesadilla in a small plastic container of sour cream and offered some to Peeps. He took a triangle. They sat in the parking lot of Dos Marcos and ate her quesadilla, sharing the sour cream. When they were finished, he remembered the packets of gum he'd gotten. He gave her the green and he kept the white. Peppermint over spearmint.

"This gum is good for like five seconds," she said.

"It's a pretty good five seconds," he said.

Kelli threw out the idea of going to get a shave ice, so he drove them to T.P.'s, a shave ice stand housed in a metal cone-shaped building that was painted to look like a teepee. They wheeled the teepee into town in the summer and sat it in the parking lot of a boarded up and abandoned motel off the dirty exit. Peeps ordered a watermelon shave ice, Kelli a lime, and they sat outside the teepee on a metal bench next to Chief Noc-a-homa, T.P.'s cigar store Indian.

Everyone called him Chief Noc-a-homa after the former Braves' mascot, even though he didn't much look like him. His skin was the color of a pecan shell and he sat on the bench with his arms folded like he was making judgments about you or the flavor shave ice you ordered. All the colors of his headdress were long faded, the look on his face grim and condemning. His nose had been sheared off. Chief Noc-a-homa was chained and padlocked to the bench as well as to the exterior of the building because kids liked to steal him and relocate him to funny places around town. It was a thing to do.

Kelli bit a big chunk from the green dome of her shave ice. "Why's the Chief sitting down?" she asked. "And not even Indian style."

Peeps looked at her to see if she was seriously asking this question. He couldn't tell. "What do you want him to do?"

"Most of the time you see these guys standing guard, like scarecrows. They scare away the white men coming to steal their land."

Peeps could hear the hum of cars on the interstate, a steady white noise droning in the distance. You could hear that sound from everywhere in Charity, one reason he liked that his dad had built their house so far out: it was a place that didn't sound like people passing by. He looked around the empty parking lot littered with trash and bits of glass, the plywood boards in the motel windows, the sign out front still bragging about free HBO.

"Who would steal this?"

"I'm having a great time. Thanks for inviting me." Kelli patted him on the back.

Peeps drank from the paper cone that held his shave ice, dripping the pink sugary juice in his mouth, sweet and cold. He crumpled the cup and thought about tossing it on the ground, but he knew better.

"You know Mitch Crandall?"

He knew she did. There'd been rumors about her and Mitch the same way there were rumors about her and Coach Gregg. Mitch had helped bring her to salvation during her crazy time. Peeps wondered why people couldn't just accept this as a good thing. Everything had to be something else. What people saw, what they observed, what actually was, was never any match for the bullshit they could imagine.

"I do," she said.

"He said something that's bothering me."

"Mitch is a cowboy," she said.

He didn't know what she meant, but it sounded like an insult.

"He says some dumb stuff sometimes." Kelli stood up and took Peeps' cup to a trash can on the other side of the door. "And he's never around when you need him."

A man and his little girl came out of T.P.'s teepee. They waved to Kelli and she waved to them. She sat across the Chief's lap and put her arms around his neck. She stuck her tongue out like she was going to lick his face. Her tongue was the color of Astroturf. Peeps thought it would make a great picture.

"Do you ever get mad about your nickname?" she asked.

Peeps thought she was asking Chief Noc-a-homa.

She asked again. "Do you?"

He shrugged. Not really. Nicknames meant you were loved. He told her that.

"No, I don't think so. Sometimes they mean you look funny or stink or no one can remember your name."

"Do I stink?"

"No."

"But I look funny."

"I didn't say that."

But he did. Just like his candy namesake. He'd gotten used to it. So what? He could be called worse. Possum was worse.

"When you leave here," she said, "nobody will call you Peeps."

She was wrong. Yes, next year he could introduce himself by his real name, say, "Hi, I'm Ben Salley." Maybe even Benjamin. "Nice to see you." But he knew eventually someone would figure it out. Around spring time, Easter, another student would be walking through the drugstore and see the candy and get reminded of the guy he sat next to in Calculus. "That funny-shaped guy! He's built just like the candy!" And then it would be back. A well-deserved nickname will come back to you. You can't shake it. You never will.

"I doubt it," he said.

"Okay, Debbie Downer." Kelli hopped off the Chief's lap, took off her glasses, and let them fall loosely on the loop around her neck. She looked at her wrist like she was checking her watch. She wasn't wearing a watch. "Why don't you just take me home so I can catch up on *The Walking Dead*?"

"One more for the road?" Peeps asked.

"Whatever." Kelli kicked a long leg at the Chief's chin.

Peeps went inside. He didn't know the boy working the shave ice machine, but he couldn't have been more than fifteen. He was skinny, a pitiful smudge of fuzz on his lip, ears the color of apples. He wore a T-shirt with the sleeves cut out and a blue T.P.'s Shave Ice visor with waves of salt stains on the band.

"Closing time," the boy said and pointed to a clock on the wall next to the door. Painted on the face was a sexy Pocahontas figure, her long black braids the hands of the clock. It was close to nine, which made it look like the wind was blowing her hair toward the west.

Steal the Chief.

The thought came to him so inevitably, so easily, like this was why they were both here in the first place, why he'd run into Kelli instead of finding Mitch, why she'd said while they were still sitting in the parking lot of Dos Marcos, "You know what would be good? Shave ice!" like she was seven years old, why he was avoiding his party. They'd been brought here together, for this. This was it.

Peeps looked around the interior of the teepee. It wasn't very big. The boy stood behind a stainless steel counter along with the robotic-looking shaving machine. Colorful bottles of flavors lined a shelf like a bar. A sink dripped water, above the sink a closed cabinet door. He needed a plan. Chief Noc-a-homa was bound to the bench and the building. He could probably set him loose with bolt cutters, but he didn't have any bolt cutters, and the time it would take to get some would be just enough time to talk him out of doing it. Kelli would know what to do—the old Kelli. She'd probably stolen the Chief any number of times. But he didn't want to tell her. He wanted it to be a surprise. Maybe they didn't have to steal it.

"How much to rent the Chief?"

The boy looked at him like he'd ordered a crap-flavored shave ice.

"I'd like to borrow him."

The boy picked up a white towel, wet it from the sink, and started wiping down the counter in wide circles. "I don't think so."

Peeps pulled a fifty dollar bill out of his wallet, fat with graduation money, and dropped it on the counter next to where the boy was mopping up. His arm stopped its circle at the cash.

The boy shook his head. "I can't."

Peeps went into his wallet again and added another fifty, as far as he was willing to go. The boy tossed the towel over his shoulder and picked up the two fifties. He held them up to the light before folding them and putting them in his pocket.

"So?" Peeps said.

The boy smiled a punkish smile. "So what?"

"I need the keys."

"Sorry," the boy said.

A mom and two blonde-headed little kids came in the front of the teepee sounding the tomahawk-chop battle-cry ringer. *Woaaaaaaah-woah-woAHohhh.* The boy took their orders and fired up the shaving machine. The mom set her purse on the countertop, digging through it for cash. She put her keys down next to her purse, a bundle of keys and trinket rings, a black vial of self-protecting pepper spray.

This was bad. This was a really, really bad idea. But here he was inside the teepee, and Kelli was outside dressed like a forty-year-old woman wondering when she could get home to watch some dumb TV show because he was boring her to death, and Mitch was still telling him *it don't get no better than this*, and his dad was at home hanging out with Peeps' friends pretending he wasn't old, and his mom was putting chicken wings on the grill because food was how she said I love you, and this punk had his hundred bucks, and there was all this, all this stuff he never did anything about and so it would just keep on happening.

The woman yelled at her two kids to stop fighting over a toy dinosaur, and that's when he grabbed her keys and ducked under the counter. The boy was surprised to see him right next to his machine, poking into the domain of those trained to work the shave ice. Peeps was quick, like throwing down to second. Minimize the moves. He had a lightning bolt for an arm. He was strong. A stream of pepper spray whizzed right into the boy's eyes.

"God Almighty!" He fell to the floor, rolling and screaming, his palms digging into his sockets. "God Almighty! Jesus! Eat shit!" The shave ice machine kept churning and shaving up ice, a lurching mechanical hum.

The woman and her two boys stood there stunned.

"Where are the keys?" Peeps yelled at the boy.

"Holy Christ!"

Peeps shook the pepper spray vial at him, threatening another dose even though the boy had curled into a fetal position and had his whole face covered now with his hands. "The keys!" Peeps yelled.

"Suck a dick!"

Peeps sprayed the boy in the back of the head and ear. His right hand shot up and pointed to the cabinet above the sink. "Please, Jesus!"

Peeps opened the cabinet. Hanging from two L-shaped pegs were two small padlock keys. He could taste the spice of the pepper spray on his tongue and could feel his index finger going hot and numb and couldn't imagine the pain the boy must've been in to have this stuff all over his face and head. Why was this even legal? He was sorry. He'd do something for him. Come back and apologize. No. The boy had his hundred dollars in his pocket. Peeps was too nice. He'd always been too nice.

The woman shielded her kids from the crazy guy shaped like Easter candy as Peeps ran out the front door with the keys. He dropped to his knees next to the bench. Kelli was still standing where he'd left her. Her glasses were back on her nose now and her arms were folded like the Chief's. The first key he tried didn't work, so he put it in the other lock, the one chaining the Chief to the building. The lock clicked open. He stuck the other key in the padlock chaining the Chief to the bench and the Chief was free. He peeked inside and saw the woman kneeling down next to the boy rubbing shaved ice in his face. His legs were kicking.

"Bad idea," Kelli said.

"Get the truck." Peeps threw her the keys to his truck and uncoiled the Chief's chains, hoping he wasn't too heavy to haul.

"This isn't going to make you feel any better."

"Get the truck!"

Peeps put one arm under Chief Noc-a-homa's legs and one under his neck and lifted him up like the Chief had been wounded in battle. He was hollow inside, light as could be. What would they do with him? Where could they take him? Kelli could come up with something—she was the artist—some fun places and poses, something nobody had ever thought of before, something original. They'd post all the pictures online. They'd be famous. Peeps felt better. Standing there holding the Chief like that he felt the best he'd felt since scoring that run, like there was possibility, like this might turn out to be a good night after all.

Kelli reversed his truck in front of the teepee. Peeps took a step forward with the Chief, ready to toss him in the bed and peel out of there when she put the truck in drive and took off, taking a left out of the empty parking lot, his white CCA baseball sticker speeding away like a homer.

Peeps' dad came and got him. He was driving Peeps' truck. Kelli must've returned it. Nice of her. The crime scene had been a joke. The cops showed up after the woman called 911. The shave ice punk accused Peeps of assault. Peeps accused the boy of stealing a hundred dollars off him, which was hard for the boy to deny, it being in his pocket. The woman said she didn't know what was going on, but she'd like a little credit for having thought fast with the relief of shave ice to the face. Her kids kept complaining that their eyes burned. The cops told Peeps that he'd used a weapon, and that was serious. They could not express how serious that was. "This is serious," they kept saying. They told the boy he shouldn't go around stealing money from honest customers and that whatever girl had caused the fight they hoped she was worth it. The boy didn't want his boss, T.P., to find out what had happened. He thought he might lose his job, so he said he wouldn't press charges, but only if he could keep the hundred dollars. This meant less trouble for everyone.

In the truck his dad didn't say a word, the way he'd always approached discipline. Silence was the sound of his father's disappointment. He didn't speak until they pulled in the driveway at the house, the yard filled with all his friends' cars and trucks, the sound of music and laughter and voices flowing over the house from the pool.

"The ice melted," his dad said and went inside.

The party was still in full swing, the music playing his dad's brand, all the kids too nervous to mess with it. His mom guarded an Atlanta Braves batting helmet filled with his friends' keys. The Keymaster, they all called her. Nobody could leave tonight. Everyone at the party waved and sang his name in the customary way, dragging out the "e." "Peeeeeeeeeeeeeeps." Peeps saw Shannon sitting on the diving board with her toes dangling in the water. She wore shorts and a bathing suit top, floral, like she hadn't realized she was back from the Bahamas. A thick rope of her hair was braided and held together with beads.

The Colonel brought him a red Solo cup full of foamy beer. He was drunk. He'd heard what had happened. "I thought I'd warned you about my sister," he said. He was in a mellow mood, his eyes half shut, smiling, exhausted probably but fighting to stay up for the party.

"Forgot," Peeps said.

They touched their cups together in a toast and the Colonel drank his down in heavy gulps while Peeps took his more slowly. The Colonel belched and bent over, burying his shoulder into Peeps' stomach like he was about to tackle him and lifted him up in a fireman's carry, spilling the rest of Peeps' beer. Peeps didn't fight. He let the Colonel toss him in the pool, let the water cool down the remaining heat of the pepper spray. The pool felt nice. When he climbed out using the ladder, he looked at Shannon to see if she was feeling sorry for him or coming to help, but she'd gotten soaked by the size of his splash and was bouncing around on her toes like he'd set her nice braid on fire. Somebody brought him a towel and he dried off and laughed with all his friends while they rubbed his wet head like a dog, good boy. He went in his room to change his clothes, took off his shirt and shorts, and pulled out Kelli's drawing, now wet and disintegrating. He tried not to think about it, tried not to get upset, tried to tell himself it didn't mean a thing.

Adult Teeth

Lately I've been following this woman while jogging. I watch her dark ponytail. Her spandexed ass. The sweat shimmering on her bare lower back. In motion her ponytail is the best part. Constantly swinging. A metronome keeping time to my lust. She always stops at the same house on Augusta, where an old man — probably her old man — sits on the steps like he's waiting for her, unsettled till she gets back. She stretches her calves, the toes of her pink and white Adidas propped on the front step, and I keep jogging by. I don't do this every day. I'm not a total creep. Just some days. Like today. And today, as I'm passing, she smiles at me, and smiles are something I've been missing lately, so I turn my head to the right and smile back, and so I'm distracted, and so I don't see or hear the car coming behind me until the smile drains from her face and she yells, "Look out!" and her old man leaps off the front steps and tackles me, just as the car barrels up the sidewalk and smashes into the façade of a convenience store, or what people in this neighborhood call a bodega.

The old man's got his arm draped over me like we're cuddling. The woman hurries over and helps him up, lifts him

off the ground and escorts him by his elbow back to his steps
before she rushes inside the house. Bits of dirt and gravel stick
in my knees. My palms are slashed with pink scrapes. Nothing
more. The driver's fine, too. He crawls out of his beat-up
Skylark, waggling his head in disbelief, muttering something to
himself. I can't hear it exactly, but it sounds like he's saying,
"mother ... mother ... mother." I sit down on the front step next
to the old man.

"Thanks," I say.

The old man shakes his head and offers me a big, toothless
smile, no teeth at all, a gaping black hole of a mouth. His face
looks like a wadded up paper sack. He stares at the Skylark,
then at me, and says something that doesn't make any sense, a
warbled groan of worry or pain or surprise or lament, maybe all
of them.

"Thanks," I say again.

He just keeps talking, the words different this time, but still
nonsense. I nod like I understand. Sirens are coming. The
woman must've run inside to call for help.

The driver of the Skylark heads inside the bodega like he'd
meant to do this, parked his car this way so he could go inside
for some chips and a Bud Light Lime. The old man digs his hand
into the front pocket of his pants and pulls out some fingernail
clippers, starts clipping his nails right there on the step. This
seems weird to me, too. His nails are shiny, like the inside of a

seashell, obviously a point of pride for him, more so than his teeth.

The woman comes back out and gives us both ice water in short plastic cups. My cup is some kind of kid's cup, likely from a fast food chain wrapped up in a movie promotion. Googly-eyed animated monsters, their colors faded, stare back at me from the cup, their eyes pleading not to be put in the dishwasher anymore. She asks the man something in Spanish, and he responds in what I assume is Spanish, his gibberish still indecipherable amid the snip of his fingernail clippers.

She places a warm hand on my cheek. "Are you okay?" she asks me.

I have actually not felt this alive in a really long time. I tell her I'm fine. "Tell him thanks," I say.

"You don't know how to say *thanks* in Spanish?" she asks. "Everybody knows that."

I remember suddenly that I do, of course, know how to say *thanks* in Spanish, but I don't say it. I take a drink of water, draining the cup, then set the googly-eyed monsters on the step, stand up, and jog back home like none of this ever happened.

▼▼▼

My wife's been depressed ever since we lost the baby, understandably, and her sandwich shop hasn't been doing so great either, the market for gourmet vegetarian sandwiches not as robust as one might figure. I try to tell her that it doesn't matter, not financially at least. We're solvent. I invested in the sandwich shop just so she'd have something to do. Before she got pregnant we thought she couldn't get pregnant, and if she couldn't get pregnant, if she couldn't do what she'd convinced herself was her prescribed role as a "woman," then she wanted something else to do. Here, I said. Make sandwiches.

Given the shit we've been through I hesitate telling her anything about my jog, but when I get home she sees the scrapes on my palms and knees, one on my elbow I hadn't noticed.

"Did you fall?" she asks.

I tell her no, I didn't fall. I almost got hit by a car, a Buick Skylark to be specific, but a toothless old man jumped off his front steps like an angel and pushed me out of the way.

"Sounds like a dream," my wife says and places her hand on my right arm, just above the scrape on my elbow and squeezes. Her hand is so cold. "I told you not to run with earbuds," she says.

When you lose a kid, or in our case come close to having one without really having one, you of course experience the typical emotions, the grief, the sadness, the loss, the thoughts of how what could've been has now changed to what is, but then there's this atypical emotion, a big one you can't help, one that creeps in uninvited. Relief. Relief at never having to see her fail, see her fall off a bike or skis, see her arms self-cut in ribbons because some punk ass didn't ask her to homecoming, hear a call in the middle of the night from the cops after her deadbeat, alcoholic husband beats her for the last time. We've been saved, in a way, spared is more like it. But thinking this way or letting these thoughts stick around for more than a second makes me feel like a psychopath. But they are there, and they are real, and I don't know what to do with them. So what do I do? I imagine she's here.

Seven months old now. At seven months she'd just begin to understand object permanence, the rather complex yet fundamental idea that a toy or a pillow or a person still exists even if she can't see it.

I still read the emails I get from BabyCenter.

That night, after my close call, I can't sleep. I get out of bed for a glass of water and go into what was supposed to be my daughter's room. We'd bought a glider and painted the walls a buttery yellow and velcroed a noise-making plush sheep to the side of her crib, a Sleep Sheep that mimics one of four different sounds: Mother's Heartbeat, Spring Showers, Ocean Surf, and the weirdest and saddest of all, the deep sea bellowing of Whale Songs. Sometimes I sit in the glider and fall asleep until morning when I wake up feeling like an exhausted parent, sore and cranky from a night spent sleeping in a chair. I had looked forward to feeling this way. I dial the Sheep to Ocean Surf and sit with my water and glide in the glider. I can see her there in the crib. She's sleeping on her side with a finger in her mouth, just as toothless as that old man who'd saved my life, only she'd never get any, and he'd once had all his.

▼▼▼

So I go back to their house. The old man is on his front steps again, and he has what's left of an unlit cigar poking from his mouth. The woman's not with him this time. A boy has taken her place, a young boy, maybe twelve or thirteen, I can't really tell. He's wearing blue jeans and a puffy black jacket. The man has on khaki pants and a short-sleeved shirt that has to have been white at one time but is now some dingy grayish yellow, the yolk of a badly boiled egg.

I raise a hand and say hi to them.

The man gums his cigar and nods.

I figure this slobbery cigar chewing is how he'd lost all his teeth. I can't tell if he really recognizes me as the man whose life he saved or if he's just being neighborly. I wish the woman was here. She'd remember me.

I try to remind him who I am, loudly and slowly, as if the old man is deaf and dumb.

"I would … like to thank you … for … saving … my life."

Neither of them move from the steps or acknowledge that I've even spoken.

"I'm offering … to get … your teeth fixed," I say.

The boy looks at the man, still gnawing on his cigar, then back to me. "He has no teeth."

"Don't you think he'd like some?"

The boy smiles. He has one of his own teeth missing and points to it, proud he's moving up in the world, soon to have a full set of adult teeth. He stands up and hops off the bottom step. "He wants cigars. And a *Playboy*. And a bag of Takis and some beer." The boy grabs my arm and hustles me toward the bodega. "Muevete."

I pull my arm away and stop. "Can I talk to him?"

"No habla ingles."

"Can you translate?"

"No."

"Can you try?"

The boy unzips his jacket as if translation is going to be a chore that requires him to be less encumbered. He sits next to the man and says something to him in Spanish, and the man looks at me and points with the wet end of his cigar, now slobbered down to a muddy nub. He's got glossy spit all over his lips, threaded between their cracked edges.

"Doesn't want teeth," the boy says.

I don't believe him. The boy hasn't told him what I've actually offered. I can tell. I try a different angle. If he doesn't want teeth, fine, I just figured that was the most obvious thing, but I'm going to do something for him. "Is there anything else he might like?"

The boy translates. The man lets the cigar fall from his lips. He stands up slowly and stomps on the cigar with a dirty white sneaker, the laces untied and stuffed back into the shoe under his gray wool socks. The wet brown smudge of his eaten cigar looks like roadkill.

The man babbles to the boy and rubs him on the head before taking the steps slowly to the front door.

"A bird," the boy says.

"What's that?"

"A bird. A parrot. He wants a parrot."

This wish is harder to read. Dirty magazines and beer could be on the boy's wish list, but a parrot?

"How do you say *parrot* in Spanish?" I ask him.

"I don't speak Spanish."

"I just heard you speaking Spanish."

"*Cotorra.*"

I'm not sure, but I don't remember hearing either one of them say this word. Maybe the boy's calling me a *cotorra*, insulting me.

"*Cotorra?*"

"Not like you say it."

"He wants a parrot?"

The boy shrugs. "Someone to talk to," he says.

My wife and I order takeout sushi because she says she wants sushi but doesn't feel like going out for sushi. I tell her I went back to see the toothless old man.

"What for?" she asks.

"I owe him," I say.

She refills her glass of wine and dips her tempura roll wildly in a bowl of soy sauce tinged green from heavy doses of wasabi. "Because he 'saved your life'?" she says, using air quotes around the words *saved your life* like that wasn't what he'd done or like it's the name of a sandwich at her shop. All her sandwiches have vaguely prescriptive names like that, the "Quick Fix," the "Hair of the Dog," the "What the Dr. Ordered."

"He did … 'save my life.'" I use my own air quotes to indicate that I believe her air quotes are excessive. I suck on a piece of edamame. "He wants a parrot," I say.

"Who?"

"The man."

"What's his name?"

"I haven't bought one yet."

"The guy, not the parrot."

"I don't know."

She puts more wasabi in her bowl of soy sauce and stirs briskly with a chopstick. "So he saves your life and you don't even know his name. You want to buy him a parrot and you don't even know his name. How about you find out his name? Maybe that's all you owe him. Maybe it's enough to walk by his steps and treat him like another human being. Call him by his name, say, 'Hello, Pedro, Jesus, Miguel, Pablo, Ronaldo—"

"You're being kind of racist now."

"Luis, Jose, Lorenzo—"

I know what this is about. She'd wanted to give our daughter a name. I didn't. I felt like I could process the grief more easily if she didn't have a name. We had one picked out, but the one we picked out was for a girl who lived. What if we have another? Why waste a perfectly good name? I'd said this out loud to her at the hospital. I immediately regretted it.

"Carlos, Alberto, Jorge ... What are some other Mexican names?"

"I think he's probably Puerto Rican."

She stops stirring the soy and gulps from her second glass of wine. "What are you so guilty of you feel like you need to save everyone?"

"He saved *me*."

"Tell him 'thank you.'"

This sounds sarcastic, like she isn't really thankful for what he'd done. Besides, I'd already told him thank you. "Do you wish he hadn't saved me?"

"No." She closes her eyes and takes a deep breath, holding it in for a beat, two beats, until she exhales, the words sailing out on her breath. "But sometimes I wish they hadn't saved me."

▼▼▼

The exotic bird store is in this nondescript warehouse building with the store's name spelled out in primary colored blocks above the wide double doors: FEATHERS. The place is filthy, the floor thick with feathers and slicked in spots with dark green and white layers of crap. None of the birds are in cages. Birds are flapping and flying everywhere, whizzing by my head, splashing in gurgling stone bird baths, clinging to perches woven from thick rope and pecking seeds from hanging feeders. The owner of the place is a short fat man who's rather birdlike himself. His white T-shirt tucked tightly into his black shorts accentuates his gut, making him look like a penguin. The sound and stink in the warehouse are both overpowering, so he tells me to watch my step and leads me to a small sales office where we can hear each other better.

He tells me what I probably want is a budgie, the most popular domesticated parrot, but he doesn't have any budgies because budgies are boring.

I ask him what he does have in the way of a parrot.

"You don't want a parrot," he says.

I assure him I do want a parrot. I tell him it's a gift for a friend of mine.

"Some gift," he says. "Do you know parrots can live to be over eighty years old?"

I tell him no, I'm not aware of this.

"Do you know how many times a week I get called to fetch some poor dead bastard's parrot? The bird left shitting itself and yanking out its feathers because its owner up and croaked?"

"Do you have any parrots to show me?"

The man waddles over to a standing nut dispenser and twists the knob, spilling a handful of cashews into his open palm.

He offers me some. No thanks. He pops the nuts in his mouth and talks while he chews. "I have one parrot. But you wouldn't want him."

"Why not?"

"He's expensive."

"Money's not really the issue."

"Then you should buy a sports car."

The man leaves his office for a few minutes before he comes back with a gray bird perched on his shoulder. The bird's about a foot long and looks like a statue sculpted from gray and white marble. He's shaped like a parrot but isn't dazzling or flamboyantly colored the way I'd imagined. His feathers scallop down his body like gathering storm clouds, and he's got only one pop of color, dark red tail feathers, that's it.

"An African Gray," he says. "Rare bird. Smartest of the psittacines."

Who would want a parrot like this? Part of the joy of owning a parrot has to be admiring its color, nature reminding us of its true vibrancy. Maybe what this African Gray lacks in color he makes up for with speech. "What's he say?"

The man rolls his eyes. "You know parrots don't really talk like we talk," he says. "They mimic. It's not like they understand what they're saying really, like they really get it. Sure, you can teach them more words, but they'll never write a play or anything."

"I'm not looking for the bird to write a play."

"Right. Right. You want him to quote your favorite movie and curse at your houseguests."

The bird sits stoically on his shoulder, looking wise, almost with a knowing grin on his sharply curved beak. He may not be colorful, but the more I watch him, the more I feel like his personality will make up for his lack of color. He has a certain presence, an aura, I guess you could say.

"How much?" I ask.

"Fifteen hundred dollars."

This is a lot to pay for a bird, an absurd amount really, but in exchange for saving my life it seems paltry. "He's going to have to talk or something before I spend that kind of money."

The man turns his head toward the bird on his shoulder, puckers his lips and makes a kissing noise. The African Gray shivers and extends his neck, placing his beak on the man's lips as if to kiss him, but the bird still doesn't speak.

"Hmm," the man says. "Usually he's a Chatty Cathy after that." He shrugs. "He'll talk when he's got something worth saying."

Because I agree to buy the bird without first hearing him speak, the man throws in a tall gold cage, a ten pound bag of unsalted mixed nuts, and a tub of calcium fortified antacids for free. Apparently African Grays need extra calcium. He also tells me that this cage won't do in the long run, and I will likely want to get him as big a cage as I can find, floor to ceiling if possible, as the African Grays are "spirited birds."

I drive straight to the old man's house on Augusta. On the way I try to get the parrot to talk by seeing if the voices of daytime sports radio might inspire him. He doesn't say anything, just sits in the back seat like stone. Nobody's on the front steps when I get there. I pull the cage out of my car and carry it up the steps to the front door, set the cage down and ring the bell.

Nobody comes.

Nobody being home had not factored into my plan. I try to peek in the front window but can't see through the gauzy curtain covering the inside. I knock on the door and wait.

The bird man told me the parrot had been left at Feathers' front door by some dead guy's family, and so the bird man had named him Lefty. Lefty's been left once; he could be left again, but I want acknowledgement that the parrot has come from me, that I've brought the old man exactly what he'd wanted as an act of thanks and repayment. Otherwise, what's the point? It'd be like leaving a tip in the tip jar when the cashier isn't paying attention.

After a second knock the old man slowly opens the door, holding the frame to steady himself. He looks terrible, nothing like the man who bravely rescued me only a few days ago. He will not outlive this bird. I tell him, loudly and deliberately, that I've come to repay the favor of him saving my life, although something like that can never really be repaid. I apologize for first assuming that he might've wanted teeth. I tell him I went to an exotic bird store and point to Lefty in his cage. All of this before remembering the man has no idea what I'm saying.

But when he sees Lefty, his face contorts into an ache of happiness. He mumbles something through his toothless mouth, holds up a finger, and recedes into the darkness of the house. I look at Lefty and he looks at me but doesn't speak.

The old man comes back with the woman, her hair down now, no ponytail, long and black and shiny like still water. She's got her wrist hooked through the crook of his elbow, and her eyes are shut like she's waiting for a surprise. She's in a man's tank top undershirt, what some people inconsiderately call a "wife beater." No bra. Her dark brown areolae whisper under the cotton like coins at the bottom of a wishing well.

The old man mumbles again, and the woman opens her eyes to behold the stoic majesty of the African Gray parrot.

She clasps both hands over her mouth and squeals. She kneels down to Lefty's level and whistles at him. Lefty perks up, flapping his wings and twisting his neck. She whistles some more at Lefty, and Lefty performs the same move he performed at the warehouse, stretching his neck toward her puckered lips.

"He wants a kiss," I say.

The woman leans forward and kisses Lefty through the gold bars. I wish I was Lefty.

"Te quiero!" Lefty shouts, his voice deep and oddly human. "Te quiero!"

"What's he saying?" I ask.

The woman stands up and looks me in the eye, and I swear she says it in slow motion, her lips glistening and her pink tongue flashing like a lure. "I love you," she says.

The old man puts his hand over his heart and laughs, his toothless mouth open and black and full of joy. The woman laughs too and wraps the old man in a hug, the two of them enjoying this remarkable gift.

I imagine the three of us, me, Lefty, and this gorgeous woman, together, bridging the cultural expanse, setting off to Puerto Rico, starting over, a new family. We would open up a small boutique hotel on the beach where Lefty would act as our mascot and sideshow attraction, his legend written up in travel guides and popular blogs. I'd learn how to surf, let my skin darken, perfect a piña colada that our guests would refer to as the best they'd ever had.

"Te quiero," Lefty says again, this time more suavely, intimately, full of romance. He looks like he's smirking at me, his beak curling toward the yellow ring of his eyeball. What a bird.

I pick up the cage and run to the car.

"Alto! Alto!" the woman yells. But I don't speak Spanish.

I tell my wife the old man hadn't really wanted a bird after all, that the boy was just playing a joke on me, so instead of taking the parrot back to the store, I've brought him home for her, for us. My wife and I have never owned a pet before because she always feared I'd get too attached, that I'd be one of those people who'd opt to give my fourteen-year-old cat stem cell treatments or expensive chemotherapy. She's right. A bird wouldn't normally be our first choice for a first pet, but Lefty's not a normal bird, and I can prove it. I tell her to pucker her lips next to his cage, and when she does he stretches his beak to her and kisses her, but he doesn't say anything.

"He talks. I swear."

She's not impressed. She stands there giving me a look, her look of pity, bottom lip drawn into a thin line, chin scrunched, her head ever-so-slightly shaking, like a bobble-head on top of the washing machine.

"These things never die," she says.

"I thought you might like a pet."

She puts her hand on my cheek. "You thought he might fix everything."

I tilt my head into her palm and close my eyes.

"You're so predictable," she says. She hugs me and buries her head in my chest. At first I think she's crying, but her body isn't radiating heat the way it does when she's crying, and there are no wet, warm tears through my shirt. She's laughing, and it feels so good to hear her laugh. I put my nose into her hair and take a deep breath in.

"I love you," Lefty says in his suave bird voice.

That night Lefty's loud in his cage, letting out random squawks and rattling the gold cross bars with his beak and claws. He won't shut up. My wife and I had disagreed over decisions to be made before we really even had to make them, and one disagreement we'd had was over sleep training, how we would prefer to help our baby sleep once she grew old enough not to need us in the middle of the night. My wife favored extinction, a method where you let the baby cry herself to sleep no matter how long it takes. Some doctors say it's the best way. Sounds cruel to me, so I argued for letting her sleep with us, believing wholeheartedly in the comfort, safety, and warmth of the family bed. Do you have to treat parrots the same way as babies? Let them cry it out or bring them into bed with you? The internet tells me neither is the right move. Parrots take in a lot of information during the day, and throwing a shroud over their cage helps them shut everything out and calm down so they can get their much needed rest.

So I get a beach towel from the linen closet and toss it over Lefty's cage, but he keeps on chattering and squawking. I carry the covered cage into my daughter's room and set it in her crib. I dial up the Whale Songs on the Sleep Sheep, believing for some reason that the sound of another animal will settle him down or that his gift with languages will make him capable of interpreting their songs. I sit in the glider and listen to the bellows, the chirp and warble of these giant beasts, their keening cries communicating something ineffable, and as I do, I wonder how in the world this sound is supposed to be soothing to anyone, much less a baby alone in the dark.

Florida Power and Light

Ed sat on a bench near the pond and kept an eye on the alligator. On the sidewalk path, Bobbi Camp-Greene walked her new dog on a leash, a puppy identical to the one that'd been eaten, maybe a tad smaller, black and white, its big ears pointed at the sky like palmetto blades. Bobbi liked to have Ed sit down on a white plastic stool in her shower so she could ride him while hot water from the hardest massage setting pelted her in the back.

Wilson crept up to Ed and sat down next to him on the bench. "We're running out of time," Wilson said. "It's a luau, for Christ's sake. What would you have us eat, Ed? Pimento cheese and Saltines? Cans of black olives?"

"Gator," Ed said. He pointed to the small alligator still basking in a patch of sun at the edge of the pond, a patch of sun near the sign that Wilson had staked, the sign prohibiting all the residents of Sundial from doing what they might have a hankering to do in a pond, swim or fish or both. Ed checked to see if Bobbi and her puppy had gotten any closer. He'd shout after her. Warn her. But she and her dog had vanished.

"I got this," Ed said.

He ran back to his E-Z-Go golf cart parked by the curb. Ed could get everywhere he needed to go in his E-Z-Go golf cart. Hadn't started his truck in a month. Sometimes this was all right. Sometimes it felt like he was the warden of a very special prison for those of advanced age and minor perversions. Sundial was connected by a series of un-busy streets to a strip mall full of convenience: Starbucks and T.J. Maxx and Publix and an oyster bar (Aw Shucks!) and a dozen other stores to get everything you'd need. Even a fake tan. Weird, given how readily available a real tan was if you spent any amount of time outdoors. That's what Ed had loved most about being a lineman, working outside, even in shitty weather, heat so bad he felt like he'd combust, soaked to the bone, wind-chapped and petrified, at least he wasn't sitting on his ass in an office. He was performing vital work, life-saving work, getting people's lights back on.

He'd customized his E-Z-Go with a tool box/cooler. The right lid of the toolbox/cooler opened to the tools, and the left lid of the toolbox/cooler opened to the Coors. The right lid hadn't seen a lot of action of late, but a few tools of his trade were still there: an old pair of insulated rubber gloves, electrical tape, rope, all resting and waiting for an opportunity to be pressed into service again.

Ed dug a fingernail under the tape edge and peeled it back so he'd be able to yank it with his teeth once he held the reptile's jaws closed. He tied a slipknot in the end of the rope and slid his gloves on, gloves rated for 36,000 volts, gloves that could surely hold down a four foot gator — five at best. He'd lived and worked in Florida his whole life. Had seen this done once when he and Ernie Young were on a service call down near Cassava. Found one waiting for them in a drainage ditch. Ernie had seen to that one; Ed had never wrestled one on his own. First time for everything. Even at sixty-eight.

Ed walked down the bank toward the alligator. Slowly. Careful not to scare it back in the water.

"A little help," he said.

"You're not serious," Wilson said.

"It's a baby."

"Baby with teeth."

"You're worthless."

"Why don't you help us all out and fetch that dead pig instead of this very much alive alligator?"

The creature was bigger, wider, and longer than he'd originally thought. Not too long ago scalybacks had all but been wiped out in Florida till some naturalists helped keep them around. Florida was full of crazy wildlife stories, pythons in bathtubs, emus causing traffic jams. After Hurricane Andrew, Ed had found a macaque fried from a downed primary that'd dropped into the monkey's live oak. A macaque.

"You are the only resident who knows how to properly barbecue this pig," Wilson said, still sitting on the bench. No help at all.

I am also the only resident who knows how to properly pleasure your wife, Ed thought.

What if Evie came out for a walk with Charlie and this gator snatched him right off the leash — Pomeranian popcorn? Why did this gator get to move about Sundial freely? Why did Ed have to warn all the residents not to take their leisure walks around the pond, the pond built for them, the pond they all loved to circle and circle and circle? This gator did not pay HOA fees. Ed did.

"And your sauce, Ed. Your sauce has won competitions!"

He crept closer to the gator. His heart thrummed like a hummingbird, and his palms dewed up inside his gloves, like hovering over extra high voltage, exhilarated in a way he'd seldom been since retiring from the bucket.

He took another step.

The gator shifted in the grass, lifting its snout toward the water, the first time he'd seen it move.

Ed looked back to Wilson.

Wilson leapt off the bench. "Watch it, Ed!"

Ed didn't turn around to see what was happening. He didn't need to. He ran, his flip-flops skimming the manicured blades of St. Augustine grass. He ran straight up the bank and to the bench, surprised at his speed. He wheezed and sputtered. His chest closed up. Arms tingled. Ed's bones had relocated themselves to places they didn't belong. A patella in his hip. A rib in his spine. He collapsed on the bench next to Wilson who could not stop laughing, slapping his knee, laughing at Ed.

Ed was nothing but a stiff dick for the widowers and the chronically unpleasured residents of Sundial Townhomes, a role he neither invited nor cherished but tolerated as some sort of special burden, or in the best of terms, a gift. With great power comes great responsibility. He'd never married. Married to his job, as they say, but in his retirement, with all this time, nothing but time, an endless stretch of blacktop time, he longed for a partner. He wanted to lie under the covers at night while her long toes rubbed the arch of his foot, the blue glow of the television tuned to a home renovation show he had no interest in watching. He wanted to complain about the way she loaded the dishwasher, suffer her nasty habits: hair in the drain, an addiction to foul-smelling cough drops, weak coffee, knuckle cracking. He wanted someone to hold his hand at the doctor's office. He wanted to know her secrets and share a few of his own, like how this gift was bestowed upon him in the first place.

It was after Hurricane Jeanne, a storm that knocked out power to over a million people across Florida, directly on the heels of Hurricane Frances, the fourth state of emergency in six weeks. Ed started to believe work would be his fate forever, getting the power back on, an inexhaustible task both rewarding and crushing, each success met by another disaster. He felt wet and swollen, a fatigue that seeped into his brain and drowned him, bred swarms of mosquitoes that sapped his blood, erupted with mildew that rotted in his ears and in the crevices of his elbows and knees. He was a bloated corpse on a pole, a feast for buzzards. There were not enough men, not enough time, yet work got the lights back on, slowly, everywhere, and despite feeling like a sunken ship, these were the times that Ed loved his job most. When nature took every man down, there were some who rose up to get things going again, to say, *hey, look here, we've made light, we've harnessed electricity, and not even a storm will take this away from us.* He thought of himself as a hero, and so did every other lineman he ever knew. All of them, if they were any good, lived for the times when nature was at its worst, and that year she'd been at her worst.

The woman lived out in Willet Springs in a log cabin down a rutted dirt road that'd been flooded in the rain that lasted days. Crews couldn't get to her, and when they finally did, he and his apprentice Luis, she looked no worse for being stranded and powerless. She wore a white robe, clean as snow, barefoot with thin ankles, toenails painted red hot as boiled lobster. She held a tall plastic tumbler in her hand with a fly fishing lure encased in its insulated walls. A Bloody Mary. A Bloody Mary she offered to Ed and Luis when they arrived.

"Been waiting three days for y'all," she said. "I'm almost out of V-8."

She had a blue and white Igloo cooler on her porch where she'd tried to salvage her refrigerator items. She'd told them all her meat was lost except what she could eat. She'd been grilling rib eyes and boar sausages as they thawed until she was sick of "eating like a leopard." The ice in her cooler had melted, but she said it was still cold.

The job was simple, and Ed felt bad she'd been out there so long for such a small problem. A tree had knocked out her service drop and had damaged her weatherhead, which he wasn't supposed to work on—the weatherhead being the customer's property—but he was already there, and it wouldn't do her much good to get her service drop hot when her weatherhead was beat to shit, so he did her a favor and fixed everything.

She sprang on her toes and clapped when the lights came on.

Ed left Luis to clean up. He wanted to see her up close again, the woman in white with the red hot toes. He walked up the front steps of her porch and took off his brain bucket, holding it against his hip.

She was gorgeous. White-blonde hair cut in a vintage Marilyn Monroe kind of style, bouncy and wavy and pert. She reminded Ed of Marilyn, not the memorialized Marilyn, but one who possibly lived on, a Marilyn who grew older with beauty and grace into a sort of indeterminate late-life agelessness.

Maybe it was the white robe. You were always seeing Marilyn in a white robe.

"I should give you something," she said.

"It's our job."

She held up a finger telling him to wait a second. Her red nails matched the color of her red toes. She went inside her log cabin, now all lit up. Maybe Marilyn Monroe had found the fountain of youth out here in Willet Springs. Maybe she was hiding James Dean in the back bedroom, Natalie Wood on a sofa bed, all the lost souls gone too early crashed in Florida. Maybe Elvis was in the kitchen. He took a step forward and peeked inside her house. All pretty standard stuff, a typical living room set and coffee table, something that looked like a church pew, but nothing totally unexpected or mysterious.

She came back to the door with two mason jars, one filled with bright green pepper jelly and the other with a clear liquid glinting in the freshly restored lights.

"I make this," she said. "Got enough to survive a lifetime of hurricanes."

She handed him the pepper jelly but held on to the other jar.

"This too. But don't put it on a cracker."

She handed him the clear jar.

"Puts the screw in screwdriver," she said and winked at him.

Ed wanted right then to go inside with Marilyn and have her run a blow dryer all over his soaked skin until he forgot what wet was, put on another one of her robes, drink whatever was in that jar and eat her pepper jelly on a block of white cream cheese with some Triscuits. He wanted to get drunk with her and lose his mind and get lost in her smell, in the pure whiteness of her skin, like diving into a vat of Cool Whip, and he wanted to wake up with her in the morning in her bed full of pillows and sweet clean sheets and have her turn over and flip the bedside lamp on, and they would both know that the only reason that lamp was shining was because of him. He'd done that. He'd brought the light.

But Ed just took the two jars, told her thank you, and left with Luis in the truck.

"*Qué chingados?*" Luis said.

Ed had never been back, although he could tell anyone exactly how to get to that log cabin in Willet Springs.

He kept the jar of bug juice in his E-Z-Go with his tools. A teaspoon was all he needed. The first time he took a hit was with a woman named Ursula he met at a bar called Loggerheads down in Siesta Key. It made him feel like lightning, elemental, wild and natural, his body lifted outside consciousness to a plane of pure electricity, power and pleasure and unflagging strength. He could lift a truck. He could rip a phone book in half. He could screw for hours. Populate a small village. Ursula asked him if he was a werewolf.

But now Ed was down to his last drop, a lonely liquid glint in the bottom of the jar, one small sip for mankind. He was saving it for Evie.

▼▼▼

Evie took Charlie for a walk around the pond every morning at 9:15, after her morning yoga. Ed wouldn't wait for her every day because he was never that obvious, and on the days he did wait for her, sometimes she did no more than wave to him while he sat on the bench. But this morning she circled the pond with Charlie, then sat down next to Ed, lifting her dog into her lap. She wore orange yoga pants and a gray hooded sweatshirt and had her hair pushed back with a tie-dyed headband. She smelled like ripe mangoes. He wanted to know the source of that smell. Did she love mangoes? Or was it her lotion? Perfume? Something he could buy at Walgreens?

"Tell your husband I'll get him his damned pig tomorrow," Ed said.

"He told me what happened." Evie laughed. "Said he'd never seen you run that fast. Even after a free breakfast buffet."

"You think it's funny?"

"You running away from an alligator that you're stupid enough to believe you can catch? Yes. I think that's funny."

"I could catch it," he said. "I could catch it for you."

"I don't recall saying I wanted an alligator."

"What is it you want?"

Evie scrunched up her nose and let Charlie lick it. She talked to the dog, not Ed, using that puppy dog voice of hers that made her sound like a cartoon character. "What's a lonely girl want, Charlie? Jewelry? A motorcycle? A hundred toes? Flowers?"

"Flowers die."

"So do alligators."

Charlie barked and hopped out of Evie's lap, charging down to the edge of the water near the sign like he'd spotted something. Evie hurried after Charlie and Ed hurried after Evie. She scooped up Charlie and held him like a football.

Bobbi Camp-Greene was walking her new dog again. She waved. They both waved back.

Ed checked around for what could've spooked Charlie. Nothing was there but that sign, the sign telling them all what they couldn't do with this pond, this pond built solely for them, the residents, not for gators to roam free and eat all their dogs.

"Wanna get naked and go swimming?" he asked.

Evie shook her head. "You'll get leeches."

Ed kicked off his flip-flops, his shirt, his shorts, down to his underwear. He yanked the sign out of the grass and walked into the pond with the sign under his arm. He kept expecting the bottom to fall out, a sheer drop, his toes losing their grip in the slippery algae-covered slick. Never happened. He could walk, never more than thigh deep, all the way out to the fountain.

Bobbi had stopped now. A blue plastic bag covered her free hand. Her new puppy was taking a dump.

Ed stood under the arc of the fountain. Let the spray rain down on his head. If he had a bar of soap, a rag, he could wash up out here. The sign said nothing against showers. He held the sign like he was picketing, the water sluicing down his face and filling his ears with a hush. He sucked water through his lips. Tasted green. He blinked through the water and saw Bobbi bend down and pick up her new puppy's small pile of shit. She would carry it all the way home. Cherish that shit all the way home to her trash, cupping the warm, soft turd like a treasure.

Ed let the sign go and watched it float in the currents stirred by the fountain. A duck shook its head at him. Ed floated on his stomach, the water just deep enough for him to keep his head up, and cruised through the water towards Evie, still standing where he'd left her. He crawled up the bank on all fours. The grass soft on his knees and hands. The sun already baking his back. He stopped in front of her.

Charlie barked. Evie smiled.

"You gonna eat me?" she asked.

Ed opened his jaws wide, ready to snap.

Ed stood at his front door wearing nothing at all. His curly white hair sprung all over his flesh like an exploded mattress. He sipped from his mug of coffee and stared at Wilson, who stood across from him dressed in black sweatpants and a black T-shirt, tucked in as to accentuate his man-boobs. Dude needed a bra. One black wristband was pushed halfway up his left arm. Ed knew they'd been doing yoga together, Wilson probably downward dogging with his nose stuck in Evie's ass.

"It's dangerous to swim in the pond," Wilson said. "It's why the sign's there. For the safety of our residents."

"Thank you for your concern." Ed sipped his coffee. He could tell that Wilson was trying hard not to look down, trying hard not to get a peek and size himself up.

"Get the pig, Ed." Wilson walked away.

Ed slammed the door.

He took his coffee through the kitchen and out to the screened-in patio. The straps of his deck chair cooled his ass. He always walked around his townhome naked. Because, well, because who was there to tell him different? Wouldn't it be nice to have someone there to tell him to put some damn clothes on, at least a robe? Have some decency and respect, Ed, for yourself and for others. His patio oversaw woodsy marshland pinned with tall pines, filled with saw palmettos and wild ferns. One of the reasons he'd bought the place. He wanted to feel like he was in the middle of nature even while at home. Lizards hung on the screen. Deer hovered in low morning fog. Sometimes he heard wild turkeys.

He would not get the pig today for Wilson. No, sir. Fuck that. What he would do instead was ride his E-Z-Go up to T.J.

Maxx and buy some yoga apparel, some tight pants and a tight tank top shirt, a headband to keep the sweat out of his eyes. Maybe some kind of healing bracelet or chakra beads or some other kind of eastern shit. A yoga mat. He'd show up at Evie's in the morning ready to stretch. They could all do it together. A new morning ritual. Evie could help Ed with his poses. He'd smile at Wilson while his wife had his hands all over Ed's back, his thighs, his arms, contorting him into uncomfortable physical positions.

Ed threw on some shorts and a T-shirt and got in his golf cart. Put the pedal down. Reached under the left lid of the toolbox/cooler and fished out a Coors. Popped it open. Let the suds pour over his hand. He sucked his fingers and guzzled from the can till his eyes watered. The breeze was perfect. Cool for a Florida morning. Sprinklers fired fresh water into the beds of daylilies in full flower.

Ed heard a scream.

He heard another scream and skidded the cart to a stop.

By the pond, Bobbi Camp-Greene and her dog were in a standoff with the gator, her puppy barking and barking like it could rip that reptile to pieces. The strength of an alligator no match for the heart of a Boston Terrier. They stood on the sidewalk path, the gator motionless on the bank between them and the water. Ed grabbed his tools from under the right lid. The rope. The tape. The gloves. He'd get it this time. This time nobody'd be laughing. He'd get that gator, and next time Wilson asked him where his pig was, why hadn't he gone to get the pig for the luau, *where's the pig? where's the pig? I need the pig*, Ed would say, *here's your goddamn pig!* and he'd let that gator loose and Wilson would piss his britches.

The gator was on the move now, like it knew a man to be reckoned with was coming. But it didn't retreat into the protection of the water. It took off into the woods. Faster than Ed could believe an alligator could move.

He stopped. Put his hand on Bobbi's bare arm. The dog kept barking. "It's okay," he said. "You're okay."

Bobbi nodded. In a trance.

"Shut up!" Ed yelled at the dog.

The dog stopped barking.

Ed followed the alligator into the palmettos and pines where it held the advantage, able to blend in, its armor easily camouflaged as a felled tree. Had to be careful. Not just for the gator but for all manner of creatures, seen and unseen. The thick scrub scratched up welts on his bare calves, no trail to speak of. No one he knew had ever ventured deep into the marshland surrounding Sundial. It was there just to look at, just to admire from your screened-in patios. He had no idea how deep it would go, how many acres it covered, but he kept pressing on, the canopy darkening and shielding the moist soil from the sun. Where was the alligator going out here? To more water? Probably leading him to reinforcements. A gang of giant lizards collected in a clearing.

Ed was out of breath when he broke into a sun-drenched, dry and sandy patch of land. He checked around for the alligator, for tracks, for a mound of reeds and palm husk that might be a nest, any sign of where it'd gone. Nothing but a lonely tree poked from the earth like a utility pole. Two thick branches split off from the top in a perfect T, just like a cross arm, and the crux of the branches was burned and blackened. Struck by lightning. And like an answered prayer, growing from that scorched wood was a spray of the most gorgeous flowers Ed had ever seen, a constellation of orange flowers, petals wide and shaped like tea cups, with long yellow pistils and deep green stems entwined like vines. Fireworks of oranges, blaze orange, burnt orange, sunshine, pumpkin. Some flecked with white, some spotted black, some light as dawn, dark as clay. Evie would flip. He would take a bunch of these back to Evie, and she would flip. She could find out what they were, take care of them, maybe pot them, plant them, keep them alive somehow on her screened-in patio, see them in her townhome and think of Ed. Ed would always be with her.

The flowers looked to be about twenty feet up or so, and the tree had no neighboring trees close enough for him to climb and reach over. But he had rope. And tape. And gloves. He could climb this tree. He could get those flowers. Ed found a small rock and tied it to the end of the rope. Wrapped the tape around the rock so it was secure, then tried to toss the rock-end of the rope up and over the branch. Only took three tosses. He tied a double bowline in one end of the rope. Threaded the other end through the loop. Pulled the knot up all the way to the branch. Yanked and cinched it down. He had to make sure the branch would hold his weight, so he jumped up on the rope and was held aloft, briefly, swinging from the branch like a monkey, until the branch cracked and sent Ed to his back and a large chunk of tree crashing down so close to his face that he had to roll away to keep from getting smacked. One of the flowers floated down next to his nose. It smelled like mangoes.

He stood up and picked the sand spurs from his forearms. There was another way. As close as two weeks from retirement, Ed could still scale a pole in under a minute, but that was with a climbing belt and gaffs. This would be tougher. He'd need a little help.

He ran back to his golf cart. Bobbi and her dog had fled the scene, probably scared out of their gourds that they'd have to watch Ed get eaten by a gator. Nobody wished to bear witness to human tragedy. Ed snapped open the toolbox, fetched the bug juice and tipped it back, tingling his lips and lighting up his throat. He found the clearing again and hugged his arms around the trunk. No thicker than a pole. Tate Bailey had freestyled a pole once at a Lineman's Rodeo when somebody told him he couldn't, and Tate Bailey was a notorious queer. Ed took off his flip-flops. Wrapped the electrical tape around and around his right foot, under his arch and over the top, then pulled a ribbon of tape across to his left foot where he wrapped and wrapped again, repeating the process, going back and forth between his feet, connecting them with taut lengths of rubbery tape, a foot-long band that would brace him and lift him up like the rung of a ladder. He had to resist the sudden urge to hump the tree. Not what he was here for. He slid on his gloves and held the backside of the tree and leapt high off the sand, his feet in a V, and sent the tape into the trunk with the hope it would catch, wedge in the bark, and it did. He moved his gloves up the trunk, one hand over the other, and pushed the tape off the trunk and pulled his knees up and fired the tape into the trunk again, where it caught. No problem. The juice was taking hold. Not being able to drive gaffs into the wood would normally make the climb slow going, but Ed was not normal now. He was a god. Hand over hand, knees up, send the tape into the trunk. The tree cooperated, what was left of its bark holding the tape and his feet with each leap up. Up and up, already half way there. Lickety-split. One more burst. And another. He could almost reach out and touch the blistered streaks of black, the vines trickling down. Ed pulled his knees up and thrust the tape into the bark, but this time the tape split, and Ed had no time to push himself away from the tree like he'd been taught. His feet slipped, and his legs wrapped around the tree, and the bark burned his thighs on the quick slide down.

Ed fell on his back and his breath left him. He lay looking up at the flowers, unable to catch air. The branches of the tree flapped like wings, and the whole tree uprooted and took off into the sky, wheeling up high with the buzzards. He sucked in air and remembered he'd been heading to T.J. Maxx. He rolled over on his stomach. Pushed himself up on all fours and made his way out of the woods, going back the same way he'd come in.

A hammering sound echoed from the pond, a rhythmic *thunk-thunk-thunk*, and when he walked out of the woods there was Wilson, driving a new sign into the bank with a rubber mallet. Ed could tell it was new from the fresh red lettering and the addition of an adverb not present on the original version:

FISHING AND SWIMMING
<u>STRICTLY</u> PROHIBITED

Wilson had his back to Ed and couldn't see him, determinedly driving the mallet into the top of the sign, *thunk-thunk-thunk*, obviously trying to make sure it was so deep the likes of Ed wouldn't be able to free it. Ed tiptoed up behind Wilson, slowly, quietly. Wilson stopped hammering. Took a step back and adjusted the sign, pleased with his work.

"Gator!" Ed yelled.

Wilson spun around, dropped the mallet in the grass and stumbled back on his heels, almost tripping over himself into the water.

"God almighty," he said.

Wilson sprinted away from Ed, straight to Ed's golf cart. Hopped in and peeled out, speeding off like someone was chasing him.

Who did Wilson think he was, commandeering Ed's golf cart like it was his own? Didn't matter. Ed had gotten a kick out of watching Wilson run away like that.

Ed reached for the new sign to pull it out and toss it in the pond and saw that his hand was not a hand anymore, not Ed's hand, but a claw really, five armor-plated and slightly webbed fingers reaching for a sign he would never be able to remove without an opposable thumb. He was hallucinating. Poisoned. Bit by a rattler. Dumb and delirious from the fall. Wilson must've caught a vacant look in his eyes, a wildness that made him run. Hopefully he'd gone to get a doctor.

Ed reached out his other hand, hoping to see his own hand, or at least something softer, cotton candy, a squirrel's paw. Nope. Also a claw. Funny. Ed felt absolutely like Ed, not an alligator version of Ed, but himself, able to use his hands to grasp the sign, able to sit on a bench and watch the ducks. Listen to the fountain. Ed felt like he was on his two feet, upright. Except. Yes. Now that he thought about it some more, his field of vision did appear to be pretty low to the ground, the ducks suddenly eye level.

He opened his jaws. The ducks flapped away.

Ed heard the putter of his golf cart coming. The cart stopped. Then voices. Wilson's voice. Evie's. The Carlsons': Betty and Eli.

"I'll be damned," Eli said. "Twelve feet if he's an inch."

"Ed and I saw one not too long ago. Wasn't this one."

Evie put her hand over her mouth like she was about to be sick.

Ed called out to her. The other three jumped. Not Evie. He must've made a noise. A bellow. Did he just bellow?

Ed put one claw in front of the other, like walking, like walking upright, and he moved, and the movement felt the same as it had felt as a man on two feet, only now there was a slight sensation of the grass tickling his belly, an overall awareness that he was covering a lot of ground, not covering ground as in distance, but his body covered a lot of the ground. He was a boat, as long and wide as a boat. Not a boat. An alligator. Not really an alligator either. Still Ed. Ed as an alligator. The whole world smelled like the bottom of a cooler. Metallic and fishy and green. Ed did not want to be an alligator.

Evie picked up the mallet Wilson had dropped in the grass.

"Look out," Eli said. "That bastard will swallow you whole."

"Gators don't eat people," Betty said.

"Let's not find out, Evie," Wilson said.

Evie threw the mallet at Ed. It hit him and bounced off his armor. Swim. He needed to swim. Ed peeled away from them and into the pond. Let the green water wash over his back. He didn't feel wet, but something else. Speed. Part of the water or the water itself. His eyes hovered on the surface. Watched the four of them still watching him. He couldn't hear them anymore and didn't want to. His ears … did he have ears now? He didn't know, but whatever he had was clogged, full of a steady underwater sound, the fountain splashing, muted and hushed, and other sounds, sounds he'd describe not really as sounds, but more as a presence. A hint of a wiggle. A swish. A plop. Ed was the pond, more like the pond than the gator he'd turned into. The water was dissolved in him, and he was dissolved in the water. Ed let his eyes sink under, surprised to discover he could still see clearly, even in all the murk.

▼▼▼

The pond became all he knew. He started to forget, to forget words he knew he knew, words that were easy, words he'd known his whole life, to forget people and times and directions. Wasn't even sure he was going the right way to look for Evie, but he knew he could always come back to the pond if he got lost, drawn not by memory but something else, a type of gravity.

On the way to Evie's, Ed stopped and ate a turtle. The whole turtle. Shell and all. The shell no match for Ed. He sensed no such thing as taste. The turtle was a necessity that fed a feeling, but it didn't fill it. So he ate a possum, because the possum did not know that Ed knew how possums played possum and therefore was not actually dead, even though he appeared to be. And it didn't matter to Ed anyway. Alive or dead. He craved something bigger. A deer. A hog. A dog. A bear. A panther. A man.

Evie sat framed in a panel of screened-in patio, full of worry. Ed could tell. He could see her, but she couldn't see him. He was hidden. Silent as a log while the morning heated up around him. Was it morning? A box of Kleenex and a phone were on the patio table. She wiped her eyes and blew her nose and let the wadded balls of Kleenex fall around her like rotted fruit. She was at a loss. She didn't know where Ed had gone, and Ed could tell she was racked between wanting to believe he'd left just for a spell and knowing something far more terrible had happened, the unexplainable, something nobody would ever figure out, something that words would forever fail to soothe. Ed could see all this. Could tell what she was thinking inside the screen. Could tell by the way she took a deep breath and blew hair out of her face before she went inside.

Ed thought she'd never come back, and he was just about to move on when she walked out carrying a tray topped with a coffee carafe. Wilson followed her, and they both sat at the table. Evie poured him a mug of coffee from the carafe and then filled up her own. White mugs. They were drinking from identical white mugs. She poured cream into both their mugs from a small carton, stirred them both with a spoon that Ed could hear clinking the walls of the mugs. He wanted to claw right through that screen and barrel over the patio table, scaly and green, huffing and hissing, a movie monster, Edzilla.

Wilson blew on the top of his coffee. Took a sip. His lips moved as Evie peeled a mango right there at the table. He couldn't make out what Wilson was saying, but Ed could read Evie's lips. *I know*, she said. That's what she said, *I know*. And what was it that she knew? What was it that Wilson said that got her to come to this recognition? *I love you. Ed's gone and isn't coming back. We must carry on with the luau as planned*. What was it? Evie peeled the mango, shedding its thick skin in leathery strips. Then she cut the mango into chunks, her fingers dripping with juice as the orange flesh fell softly into her husband's oatmeal. Evie buttered an English muffin and the two of them ate breakfast together. Husband and wife.

He had to let Evie know where he'd gone and that where he'd gone was not far. When she saw and when she knew, she would take him in, keep him in the bathtub as a pet, let him sleep in her bed, roll him over and rub his belly, pet him on the snout. Or. Maybe all this was just some kind of bad dream or curse, and once she knew it was him, that the gator was Ed and Ed was the gator, she could give him a kiss, wake him up and make him whole again.

The work had taken some time, days he thought. He didn't know. Days of basking next to the pond and scratching his claws at the sign, scraping away the red letters so they said what he wanted them to say. Sometimes he could see what they meant, could remember how letters arranged to configure words in a language he had known, words that meant something, but other times they looked like nothing at all, meaningless squiggles, but he kept at it, and thought he had it, and when it was time for the luau he dragged the sign in his jaws, ready to show them all.

Several white party tents were set up on the lawn next to the pool. Ed could tell that Wilson had decided to spend the association's money and have the thing catered. Workers milled about in white jackets. Set up stainless steel trays and chafing dishes. A whole pig roasted on a spit. Not the way Ed would've done it. All the homeowners were out. All of them wearing fresh floral leis and tropical shirts. All of them shuffle-dancing on a parquet floor to a band playing some kind of island song.

Ed did not see Evie anywhere. But Betty saw Ed. She was dancing with Eli when she stopped and pointed in his direction. Others followed, turning slowly, and the band stopped playing, and soon all of them were staring at Ed staring back at them.

"That's your sign," Eli said.

Wilson scurried away from the tent.

Ed took a step forward. Bobbi Camp-Greene screamed.

"Maybe he's trying to tell us something," Betty said.

Read the sign, people. Just read the damn sign. Sound it out. What's it say?

Maybe he'd done it wrong. Maybe it didn't say anything. Didn't say what he thought it said, and even if it did, would they believe it? Would any of them believe it?

Wilson came charging back. The crowd parted to let him through, and there he stood, opposite Ed at the far end of the parquet dance floor, aiming a deer rifle at Ed's snout.

Ed no longer felt like everything, a part of everything. He felt utterly alone. And scared. Not ready to take a bullet through the brain. All he wanted was to tell Evie what had happened.

The rifle stayed aimed at Ed.

Ed did not move.

"You can't do that, Wilson," someone shouted.

"Like hell."

"It's against the law."

"What is against the law is for a reptile to ruin my luau."

"This is an extraordinary animal. Is it in the wrong place? Yes. Does that give you the right to shoot it in the face? No."

Wilson lowered the rifle. "Gimme your plan then. You have one? Or maybe you want him to eat your Prius while we wait for you to figure it out."

"I don't see what my Prius has to do with this."

"I am eradicating a problem in our community."

"Call the Florida Wildlife Commission."

Wilson raised the rifle again.

"Okay. Shoot it in the face. Then what? How are you going to get this 600 pound animal out of here without anyone knowing?"

"Plan to sink him in the pond."

"And nobody will be the wiser?"

He lowered his rifle. "That's a dumb thing to say, figuring as I just told you my plan."

"Go for it!" someone shouted. And a few others applauded. Said, "Aye." As if this was a formal board meeting, which it had sort of turned into. Representatives from every townhome formed an aisle on the dance floor, lined up like Wilson and the alligator were the final contestants in a dance-off.

"You have entrusted your townhome association president to act on your behalf. Therefore," Wilson raised his rifle, "I see this as a necessary act on your behalf and in your own best interest."

"Stop!"

Evie ran out from the crowd and stood between them, her back to Ed, one hand stretched towards Wilson, and the other clutching Charlie. She was barefoot and wore a skirt patterned with orange flowers. Ed heard her say something else to Wilson but couldn't tell what it was.

Look at the sign, Evie. Turn around and look at the sign, read it, you see?

IM

ED

See it! Read it!

IM

ED

Still here! Still here! Sound it out!

IM

ED

"Evie," someone shouted.

She was still talking, her back to Ed. Not talking, but yelling. Yelling at Wilson. Giving him an impassioned speech, probably about the dignity and majesty of scalybacks. Wilson listened, the muzzle of his rifle pointed at the sky, the barrel resting against his shoulder.

Ed was eaten up with love and want.

A man stepped from the row of residents and tried to grab Evie. His eyes were white and wide, and his head swiveled from Ed to Evie to Wilson, from Wilson to Evie to Ed. "Evie," he said. "Evie. Move. You've got to move."

Ed felt himself getting closer to her, to her long and beautiful bare feet, to those toes he sucked that one time they were together. They were drinking Arnold Palmers by the pool. Wilson was at the chiropractor. Evie told Ed she loved to have her toes sucked, ticklish and a turn-on at the same time, but Wilson refused to do this for her. Said it was disgusting. In the women's changing room of the pool house, she sat on the counter with her feet in the sink and Ed washed them, gently massaging his soapy fingers between her toes before he dried them off and started sucking, slowly, the piggy that went to market, the piggy that stayed home, the piggy that had roast beef, the piggy that had none, down to the piggy squealing *wee-wee-wee* all the way home. Each piggy tasted of soap. Eventually he tried to move up her leg. His lips pressed to her smooth calf, creamy with sunscreen, up to the knee and even the inside of her thigh before she pushed his head back down to her toes and said, "Maybe another time." He could smell her now. Toes and mangoes. All of her, getting closer to him, slipping back on a conveyor toward his jaws.

The man shook her by the arm, and she jerked away from his hold, and as she jerked, she dropped Charlie. She bent down to pick up the dog, but the man grabbed Evie, this time in a hug, and dragged her kicking her bare heels across the floor. Charlie was left alone, a brown puff of protection, *yip, yip, yipping*, then charging at the gator just as Wilson aimed his rifle at Ed and fired.

The shot reverberated down his armor and through his tail and out into the wide open as the residents shuddered and covered their ears, but Ed felt nothing. Evie's mouth was open in what looked like a scream, but he couldn't hear her. The look of pain on her face made Ed want to hurt something, hurt the man holding her back, keeping her from running to save her dog. Charlie was a heap, a brown mound before him, blood slowly pooling around his still haunches. Wilson stood on the other side of Charlie, the barrel of his gun hanging limply. He was shaking his head, his eyes shut, shaking his head. Evie fell to her knees, and instead of going to her, consoling her, knowing he couldn't do that, couldn't put an arm around her and tell her he was still here, Ed dropped the sign and moved quickly to Charlie, scooped the dying dog up in his jaws, careful not to hurt him any more than he was already hurt. He tasted the blood as warmth, the life of Charlie, still with him. The man who'd been holding Evie dragged her farther away as Ed moved closer with the dog cradled in his jaws. The closer he got, the farther away everyone scattered, and he understood why they were afraid, but they didn't need to be afraid. They just didn't understand how this might mean anything other than what it appeared to mean. All he wanted was to get close to Evie, to drop the dog at her feet, take her dog to her, so she could be the one to hold him as the lights went out.

Acknowledgements

Thanks to Jerry Brennan and Lauren Gioe at Tortoise Books for their dedication to editing and publishing this collection.

Thanks to all the editors at the magazines where these stories first appeared: "Welcome to Gorilla City" in *Fifth Wednesday Journal Plus*, "Trash Days" in *Third Coast*, "Rapture" in *The Florida Review*, "Nesting" in *FRiGG*, "Leaving Charity" in *The Carolina Quarterly*, "Everything is Going to be Okay" in *Printers Row Journal*, "Inside the Happiness Factory" in *Hobart*, "Chopsticks" in *Curbside Splendor e-zine*, "Piss-ants" in *Bull: Men's Fiction*.

Thanks to all my peers and mentors at Northwestern University who helped contribute to many of these stories in no small ways.

Thanks to Michael Langley, Stuart Dybek, Patrick Somerville, Sandi Wisenberg, Christine Sneed, Emily Ayshford, Ankur Thakkar, Schuyler Dickson, and Alex Higley, for their friendship, inspiration, and insight over the course of many drafts and/or conversations.

Thanks to Super B for his amazing cover.

Thanks to Chad Evans for all his wild-eyed dreams.

Thanks to Jed for showing me I was doing it all wrong.

Thanks to my mom, dad, and sisters for always laughing.

Thanks to Sam for always wanting me to read to her and for our "secret" pancake suppers.

And thanks most of all to Shira for inviting me over for soup.

About the Author

Jeremy T. Wilson is a former winner of the *Chicago Tribune's* Nelson Algren Award for short fiction. He teaches creative writing at The Chicago High School for the Arts and lives in Evanston, Illinois.

About Tortoise Books

Slow and steady wins in the end—even in publishing. Tortoise Books is dedicated to finding and promoting quality authors who haven't yet found a niche in the marketplace— writers producing memorable work that will stand the test of time.

Printed in the USA
CPSIA information can be obtained
at www.ICGtesting.com
JSHW022322140824
68134JS00019B/1243

9 781948 954013